Sandy Remains

Sandy Remains

A Blue Diamond Mystery

Kathleen Faucett

Mystery is the spice in life —
Kathleen Faucett

iUniverse, Inc.
New York Bloomington Shanghai

Sandy Remains
A Blue Diamond Mystery

Copyright © 2008 by Kathleen F. Faucett

All rights reserved. No part of this book may be used or reproduced by any means, graphic, electronic, or mechanical, including photocopying, recording, taping or by any information storage retrieval system without the written permission of the publisher except in the case of brief quotations embodied in critical articles and reviews.

iUniverse books may be ordered through booksellers or by contacting:

iUniverse
1663 Liberty Drive
Bloomington, IN 47403
www.iuniverse.com
1-800-Authors (1-800-288-4677)

Because of the dynamic nature of the Internet, any Web addresses or links contained in this book may have changed since publication and may no longer be valid.

This is a work of fiction. All of the characters, names, incidents, organizations, and dialogue in this novel are either the products of the author's imagination or are used fictitiously.

ISBN: 978-0-595-50432-9 (pbk)
ISBN: 978-0-595-61509-4 (ebk)

Printed in the United States of America

A Special Thanks To:
Lieutenant John Goodwin
&
Officer Brett Heintz
Of The Ocean Isle Beach
Police Department

For my father Wayne and sister Molly for pushing me for more,
My mother Barb and sister Ruth for editing,
My husband Phil for his moral support,
And my Sphynx cat Blue Diamond Gizmo for his loving attendance at the computer.

This book was preceded by:
Tiwardrai On The Strand
Available through iUniverse.com

Characters

Sisters
Kate: The eldest, tends to take charge and rely on her heightened senses. Hopes to breed Sphynx Cats for a living, married to Ellsworth.

Anne: Middle child, often the peacemaker, likes hard evidence before making a decision. Plans to retire in three years and travel with her husband Keith.

Samantha: The youngest, clear headed, usually states what everyone else is thinking. Is an excellent trained reflexology therapist, married to Todd.

Husbands
Ellsworth: Survivor of two heart attacks in one day; now views life less critically.

Keith: An art major from the sixties prefers to meticulously check out all possibilities.

Todd: Fights to control his anger and questions all self-appointed authority figures.

Mother and Father: Enjoy their retirement and often take mission trips around the globe.

Blue Diamond In The Rough: A Sphynx cat whose inquisitiveness plus bold behavior never allows him to keep out of trouble or stay clean.

Chapter 1

▼

Father still had the binoculars to his eyes, unable to tear himself away from the gruesome site that was being uncovered just down the beach. "You guys are not going to believe this," he stated matter-of-factly. "Someone buried a body in the sand."

"Dad, kids bury each other in the sand all the time at the beach. Remember the time we had you covered up to your chin?" Samantha replied. Everyone was watching for dolphins through binoculars.

"No, I'm pretty sure this one is dead," Father returned as Kate and Ell came bursting out the door onto the deck.

"Something is wrong, something bad has happened," Kate announced breathlessly. She and her husband Ell had been in the kitchen getting preparations started for the evening meal, it was their day for cooking dinner.

"That's what I have been trying to tell everyone," father interjected.

"Sorry dad," Anne stated as everyone squeezed in at the railing on one end of the deck. Using their binoculars they tried to get a look before the place was overrun with people. Kate went back in the beach house to get her and Ells' so they could get a look also.

The children and dog that had uncovered the body backed away from the digging site as a woman came out to see why there was screaming. She herded the children and dog ahead of her back up to the house and returned with another adult and a cell phone. They were evidently calling the police.

An arm and a portion of the torso were now visible from the hole where the dog had been digging. The makeshift grave didn't appear very deep, as if it had been hastily dug. From what they could see of the body they judged it to be male.

"I wonder if it would be rude to go down and look at the body." Sam spoke her thoughts. "Oh, sorry, I didn't realize I said that out loud." Both her parents turned to look at Sam and her sisters giggled at her predicament. Sam swallowed self-consciously before she asked, "Do you think it would?"

Father answered, "I'm pretty sure the dead guy isn't going to care, and I think the parents of those children would be relieved to have another adult down there. What do you think dear?" He had directed the question to his wife.

"I'd say, if you can stomach the decomposing remains left by the sand crabs then go ahead, just remember the eyes are the first to go." Mother was always to the point if not tactful with her girls, she wasn't one for homicide, which this obviously was, since he couldn't very well bury himself. "Kate, don't forget you still have dinner to finish, so please don't stay over there too long, only my hips benefit when I eat late."

As the girls and their husbands headed across the deck toward the steps, mother raised her voice ever so slightly as she added, "And don't touch anything."

❦

Mothers' eyes followed the small group walking across the beach toward their destination. "Do you think we encouraged our children too much when they were growing up to investigate every situation before coming to conclusions?" Her motherly instincts had kicked in at the inquisitiveness of their children.

"I'd say it's too late for us to worry about it now, and since we survived their teen years, let their husbands monitor their current shenanigans." Father replied as he turned his binoculars toward the ocean once again searching for dolphins.

"I suppose you are right dear." Mother breathed a soft sigh and released just a small portion of her worry. She lifted her binoculars and began to scan the water's surface.

Mothers' eyes were not the only pair watching the small group cross the expanse of beach to the sandy remains. Blue was in one of the upper windows watching the events unfold below. The dog barking had woken him from a sound nap and his attitude toward it at this moment was testy at best. The sun had lulled him to sleep earlier after his romp up and down the stairs and his requirement of rest was not yet complete.

His people were now walking toward the body partially hidden in the sand. Not a very good burial if you asked him. Humans' idea of burying something was laughable. This body was merely covered, not buried; it would have been uncovered eventually by the winds if the dog had not picked up the scent first.

Blue was fidgeting on the narrow window ledge and nearly fell to the carpet below. He would have caught the scent right away if he would have been able to run loose like the dog. Cats' sense of smell pulls in more than one odor at a time because it processes at a higher level than a dog. He probably would have been able to tell how the human was killed and even who the killer was. Cats' are so superior to dogs he thought, why haven't the humans noticed that.

Blue caught the suns' reflection off of something further down the beach but it was gone before he could pinpoint its location. Someone else was watching the activity going on below. The question is; were they horrified at what they saw or satisfied with the deed?

Chapter 2

"Oh my gosh, look at his skin, what could cause that kind of damage?" Sam was quite intrigued and would have kneeled down for a closer look at the skin if mother had not just cautioned them to stay clear. They stood in a circle surrounding the dead body lying in its makeshift grave. "I wonder how old he is," Sam continued since everyone else seemed to be stunned into silence. The small group confirmed, from what was visible at this closer view, that the previous assumption of a white male was correct. The left arm was protruding out of the shallow hole at an odd angle and the dogs' teeth had ripped the skin with his canines when he had tried to pull the body loose from the sand.

"I've never seen anything like it," Anne spoke up. She and Keith had taken a step closer to the body.

Still hanging back, Kate had her hand to her mouth, her eyes staring at the multitude of divots both large and small covering the visible skin. "I think they were made by crabs," Ell volunteered, "they are such opportunists." The crabs had definitely made a feast of this body's misfortune.

The man and woman who had called the police were keeping their backs to the corpse and their eyes on the beach house. Another adult was on the deck keeping the children from coming back outside while watching for the police. The dog was in the beach house looking out the sliding door, occasionally showing his displeasure at being confined by barking.

"I hope I never see anything like it again," the woman stated rather sternly. She had originally come down to see why her daughter was screaming and discovered the body. The man with her reached up and patted her on the shoulder but kept quiet. They were vacationing this week like nearly everyone else along this strip of the beach. Very few owners live on the beach year round and almost all of them rent out the houses when they can. With no covenant codes, some of the beach houses had become shabby compared to others on the island.

Kate walked over to the couple, "I'm so sorry the children saw this, but they are resilient you know, and will bounce back to normal in no time. Their brains seem to have a way of forgetting the bad and allowing the body to recover shocks like this."

The woman whipped around to face Kate, her eyes showing hatred toward the interloper. "Who do you think you are? It's bad enough you're down here gawking at the body; don't think you can placate me with psychoanalysis babble about how my kids will handle something." Raising her hand she pointed her finger in Kate's face to emphasize each word, "You and your high fa-lootin' family, staying in that big expensive house, you're no better than we are."

"Elyse, calm down." The man standing with her finally spoke. His polished tenor voice was at chaos with its surroundings.

"Remember your blood pressure," he added, hoping to distract her long enough to get the annoying woman to walk away.

His voice finally registering in her mind as familiar and she turned toward him, "Leo, don't start with me," Elyse's voice was beginning to shake. "I ain't gonna have some high mucky-muck telling me *anything.*"

Leo's hand encompassed Elyse's left shoulder and his tenderness took Kate by surprise. He reminded her of a favorite teddy bear she had when she was young, only with a neatly trimmed beard. The small tanned creases barely visible at the corners of his eyes gave him a gentle look.

"I'm sure she didn't mean anything by it. She was only being sympathetic for what the children were subjected to," Leo explained. This seemed to quiet the woman down and her shoulders slumped forward as she closed her eyes and dropped her head. The man moved his head ever so slightly for Kate to leave as he folded his arms around Elyse in a comforting embrace.

Kate quickly retreated to her own little group, her eyes wide with tears threatening to spill over. "That poor woman is on the verge of a breakdown," she whispered. "I don't know why she doesn't head back up to the house." Kate held her hand up before her sisters had a chance to speak. It would be better to wait until they had returned to the beach house. There was no need to further upset the woman by discussing her outburst where she could hear them.

Hoping to get more information on the victim once the police arrived, they all sat down in the sand and waited. Elyse and Leo frowned when they saw them sit, but said nothing further to them.

It seemed forever before they heard the sirens signaling the police had arrived.

Chapter 3

The sheriff took Elyse and Leo's statement before allowing them to return to the deck of their beach house rental. The sisters and their husbands stood up when the sheriff arrived but remained waiting near the body until the coroner and his staff finally arrived. They moved out of the way when the coroner began processing the crime scene.

The sheriff walked over to the small group. "Were any of you witnesses to the discovery of the body?" His voice was gravelly, as if he was just recovering from a bout with laryngitis.

"Our father was; he saw the children and their dog through his binoculars digging in the sand just as they uncovered the body." Samantha stated as she pointed up at their father still sitting on the deck with their mother, watching the dolphins. "I'm sure he wouldn't mind if you wanted to ask him a few questions," Samantha volunteered.

"Yes I would, after I talk with you all," the sheriff replied as he removed his sunglasses and put them in his pocket before continuing. "What is the reasoning for you people to be standing around here, are you crape hangers or just plain nosy?"

"I take offense to that remark sheriff," Kate spoke up for the first time and stepped in front of the sheriff. Her boldness had the rest of those in her small group put a distance between her and them by taking a step backwards in tandem, a move the sheriff noticed. "We have been waiting for you *officials* to arrive so that we could give you what little information our father could offer, and you want to treat us like thrill seekers." Kate straightened herself up to her full five foot three inch height, hands on her hips and stared with unwavering eyes directly in the sheriffs' face.

The sheriff seemed taken aback. His eyes went wide and just a faint color of pink showed in his cheeks before disappearing and he regained control. "Madam, I do not know you from Adam and you expect me to assume you were only standing around to help in the investigation? I think not. We have nut jobs show up at nearly every case we have on The Strand. If you expected me to know that you are not just another one of those then you are sadly mistaken." The sheriff stood toe to toe with Kate and did not back down.

"How dare you call us nut jobs, and your manners are in severe need of realignment sir," Kate spoke through clenched teeth, she was still smarting from the tongue-lashing she had received from the distraught parent and the sheriff had just stepped too close to the line of etiquette with the wrong person, at the wrong time. Kate relaxed her jaw. Her mother had taught her to never look angry when delivering your striking blow. "I believe this is an election year for you sheriff, and if I recall correctly, that was one of your *thank you* signs we saw as we drove through town. I would hate for a formal complaint filed for your misjudgment of law abiding citizens to pop-up on your file and be the cause of you losing the election in the fall." The edge of her lips rose slightly but the smile never reached her eyes.

The blood in his face drained to the pit of his stomach, she had hit the mark she was aiming for with that final statement. It had been a close race and he still had competition in the fall. His rough demeanor crumbled "I meant no disrespect ma'am, it's been a long day and this is my first day back from an illness. Please forgive me for the accusation." His words were spoken softly, as though he was truly worn out. He rubbed his hand down over his face, as if to wipe away the stress. His gut was warning him to watch his step with this woman.

Kate felt the sincerity in the tone of his words when he spoke and allowed a softness to show in her eyes; she was not one to hold a grudge and it would not bode well for their investigation to get the locals up in arms. "I accept your apology sheriff and I'm sorry to hear of your illness, I wish you well on your mending." Ell had come up behind her and touched her elbow to let her know he was there to support her. She let out a small sigh to banish any tension that may have been left before stating, "I've got dinner to finish. My sisters will see that you talk to our father." Kate turned her back to the sheriff dismissing him from their conversation. Ell's hand slipped around her upper arm as he guided her through the soft loose sand that gathered along the ridge of sea oats growing on the dune.

"You really shouldn't have cut him so close to the quick Kate. You must have hit a nerve; he turned positively gray when you delivered that statement." Ell kept his voice low so the wind wouldn't carry his words back to the sheriff as they headed back toward their own beach house.

"I don't care Ell, he called us nosy nut jobs," Kate whispered back.

"We *were* there just to satisfy our own curiosity, he was right in that aspect and he didn't know us, we could have been nut jobs for all he knew," Ell replied.

"Well, we're not, and we can't solve the case if we don't investigate the crime scene," she informed him. "Too bad we didn't grab the camera before we headed over there, pictures would have helped us tremendously in our investigation."

Ell just rolled his eyes heavenward and shook his head as they climbed the steps to the gazebo. There was no stopping them now, he had seen that look in Kate's eyes before; she was like a dog with a bone, no pun intended to the dead guy. They stopped before going in the door and informed mother and father to expect a visit from the sheriff, and then proceeded on in the house to finish preparing the evening meal.

Chapter 4

▼

Kate was too distracted to concentrate on her cooking. Ell had to bring her attention twice back to the orange sauce that had started boiling, and she nearly burned the chicken breasts she had been searing in the skillet a moment ago. Her thoughts were not on her cooking nor were they on the dead body being removed by the coroners' staff at this very moment. They were on her previous visions of red sand spreading across this whole end of the island, fading in and out, just beyond her grasp. Shaking her head to clear the thoughts, she stared down at the bubbling orange sauce.

"I am so glad I decided to purchase that Caesar salad mix," Kate began. "I don't think I could keep focused long enough to do the salad justice if I did it from scratch. Ell, could you shred the Parmesan? Just put it in that bowl setting on top of the microwave, and if you would, spray the salad with the vinegar wash and rinse it with cold water, you can let it drain on paper towel."

"And what, pray tell, are you going to be doing while I'm doing all this?" Ell knew she had only planned on a simple dinner.

"I still have to get the risotto finished and cut up the basil for the orange sauce," Kate replied, and then added, "Could you dump the sourdough rolls into one of those bowls setting on the counter? Cover it with a damp dishtowel and add it to the hot plate next to the chicken breasts. Oh, and dear," Kate continued, "Would you set the table, then you can rest until time to eat. Thanks sweetie."

"Who was your grunt labor this time last year?" Ell whispered into her ear, and then kissed her on the neck. He had come up behind her while she was at the stove stirring the sauce and giving him his instructions for help.

"Oh," Kate replied, she would have jumped if Ell hadn't put his hands on her shoulders, he knew her too well. "Talk about distractions, and I believe my grunt labor as you call it was the same as it's been for the past thirty plus years."

"You are such a slave driver," Ell whispered.

"Speaking of which," Kate jumped into another subject, "I'd like to drive up the coast to Wilmington and go to that museum with all the history on Slaves."

"You tried to go there a few years ago and couldn't handle it." Ell reminded her. "You had broken down in tears before we got halfway through and you couldn't finish. You nearly passed out for heavens sake. I don't think it's a good idea this year, not with the murder and all."

"Perhaps you're right," Kate relented. "But let's make plans to do it next year, okay?"

"Next year, yeah, we'll try it then," Ell mumbled just to appease his wife.

☙

Kate and Ell's Sphynx cat Blue, hearing his people, had slipped into the kitchen hoping for peanut butter but would take a cuddle if he could get someone to pick him up. They were both occupied cooking, so he thought a quick jaunt up to the previously *secret hidden* room would do as a good distraction. He noticed they had not yet covered the opening under the bottom shelf in the pantry and he had such great fun exploring that room until the family finally discovered it was there and checked it out. It had thick ropes of cobwebs draped everywhere, an old wooden chair and table long past its prime with pots of paint and brushes scattered across it, a large easel with a partially worked canvas setting on it and a window that allows the wonderfully warm sun in.

Unfortunately for Blue, Kate had caught him out of the corner of her eye. "Oh no you don't mister; I do not have time to give you a bath before dinner." He was scooped up in loving arms, kissed on the head and handed to Ell, "Shut him in the bedroom." Then quickly added, "Just go ahead and lay down while you're upstairs dear, it's going to be another twenty minutes or so, and I can set the table myself. You look a little tired and I know Blue would love the company."

"This kind of grunt work I don't mind." Ell leaned over and kissed her on the forehead before he escaped the kitchen with Blue and made a mental note to cover that opening after dinner.

Chapter 5

While Kate was finishing dinner preparations in the kitchen, her sisters brought the sheriff over to speak with their father. The girls' husbands had conveniently stayed behind to watch the removal of the body from its sandy grave, with strict instructions from their wives not to miss one detail.

"Dad, the sheriff has a few questions about what you saw," Anne started speaking as soon as they hit the top step of the deck. "We let him know you had watched the children digging through your binoculars, we knew you would want to help in anyway you could."

Father had watched his two youngest daughters and a gentleman in a sheriff's uniform make their way across the expanse of beach that separated this house from the rest of the houses on the end of the beach strand. He stood and reached his hand out to shake hands with the sheriff as he introduced himself and his wife.

"Jack Robertson, and this is my lovely wife Dexie Bolton-Robertson of the East Coast Bolton's'," he stated in a brisk smooth tone.

The woman reached up her hand to the sheriff, he wasn't sure if she was offering it to be kissed or shook. He gave it a limp shake and let go quickly. "Nice to meet you both, my name is Clayton Poole; sorry we couldn't have met under better circumstances."

"Are you by any chance related to Oscar Poole out of Boston?" Dexie's interest was piqued and she had leaned forward in her chair.

The sheriff was taken aback with her voice; it was soft but firm and had a slight drawl to it, but not a southern drawl and definitely not what he had expected. "Not that I am aware of ma'am," he informed her. "We all hail from southern Virginia."

"Oh, what a pity," she replied, "I haven't heard from the Poole's in years, I was hoping for a bit of news on how the family was doing." She set back in her chair as if to dismiss him. He saw that same look in the eldest daughter's eyes just before she had turned and walked back to the beach house. It was a definite dismissal. He now knew how a servant from the early 1700's would have felt and he didn't much care for it.

The sheriff turned his head toward her husband Jack, "Your daughters tell me you were watching the children dig in the sand, do you want to elaborate on what you saw?" Sheriff Poole stepped up on the wooden bench running the width of the deck, sat on the railing along the top of the bench and leaned against a support post going up to the roof; this gave him a better view of all four people sitting on the deck. He reached into his pocket and pulled out a note pad with the pencil attached to it with a string. "I have a habit of loosing my pencils and my wife gave me this as a joke, at least I haven't lost it yet." He explained to the expectant stares, and then returned his attention to Jack.

Clearing his throat first, Jack described the events as they happened. "We had come out on the porch earlier, I'd say between four and four-thirty, to watch for dolphins with our binoculars. I gave the water a quick scan but didn't see anything. So I turned my attention to the beach and looked for more excitement than empty rolling waves. The dog was already pawing and flipping sand when the children came over to help. The deeper the hole got the more excited the dog became until he finally got a hold of the arm and began tugging. That's when the little girl began to scream. The dog didn't let go of the arm until the woman who came out to check on the little girl told him to." Father had leaned forward as he was talking, so when he finished he settled back in the rocker and waited for any questions the sheriff might have for him.

The sheriff finished writing before asking any questions. "Had the kids been digging anywhere else that you saw?"

Jack thought that an odd question but let it slide, "Not that I noticed, the dog was pretty adamant as to where he wanted to dig and the children evidently weren't that picky."

"Have the children been digging holes all week?" The sheriff continued.

"How should I know?" Father's voice was raised only slightly with agitation. "This is the first time I noticed the children, actually the dog is what had drawn my attention. He was digging so violently, as though he was on a mission."

The sheriff now knew where the eldest daughter inherited her temper, "How long are you folks staying here?"

"We're paid up through Saturday," father replied. "Why?"

"Well, if I need you to stick around longer than that I'll give you a call." The sheriff stepped down off the bench and turned to go.

"Why would we need to stay longer than that," father asked.

"I didn't say you would, but you know, just in case we run into any problems. I'll let you know before Saturday morning." The sheriff walked down the deck to the steps that led to the gazebo.

"If we have to stay," father followed him to the top of the steps to inform him, "I don't plan on paying for it so you better make sure you *need* us to stay for the taxpayers' sake."

Father didn't see the sheriff flinch at his remark, but Sam and Anne did, and so had Keith and Todd as they passed him on the wooden walkway.

Ell came out the door to let everyone know dinner was ready as the sheriff headed out through the gazebo and on down the steps to the sand. Ell pulled Keith aside, "Kate wants to meet after dinner to get all the details."

Keith nodded, "We figured she would. It was grizzly, those crabs were merciless."

Chapter 6

▼

"Kate, that rice was delicious," Keith said. "What did you put in it?"

"It's Risotto; it has four different cheeses and Rosemary." Ell answered for her. He had asked Kate earlier in the day when she had mentioned she was making it with her orange and basil chicken breasts. She had been worried the two pungent herbs would fight for attention on the palate, but they seemed to work out very well.

"Well, it was wonderful." Keith turned to his wife, "Anne, you need to get that recipe from your sister. It would go great with my grilled Mahi-Mahi."

"You are so right Keith," Anne returned her agreement. "Kate …"

"I know, I know," Kate didn't even let Anne finish her request; "You need the recipe."

"Yes, if you could, maybe later jot it down for us." Anne's eyebrows were raised in question, waiting for her answer.

"Ooooh, write one out for me too," Sam jumped in on the request before Kate had time to tell them she would or wouldn't. And of course, mother wanted a copy also. Secretly Kate was thrilled to have them ask, the others were excellent cooks in their own rights.

"You know Kate," mother began, "This evenings' meal was delicious, and although we did end up eating a tad later than usual, I refuse to let it settle on my hips. So Jack dear," mother turned to her husband, "We are going for a moonlit walk, not far of course, but far enough to get my metabolism kicked in."

"Oh absolutely," father replied and then winked at her, "Any excuse to get my lovely wife all to myself."

"We'll need our jackets," mother scooted back her chair, "Do you want to walk barefoot?"

"No, I think it will be safer for our toes with water shoes, the crabs will be coming out," he reminded her as they stood up and both headed toward their room to change shoes.

The rest of the group began clearing off the table. "Thanks for helping; I can't wait to find out everything that happened while I was cooking dinner." Kate told them.

"We knew you would," Anne smiled, "Well, that and Ell told Keith you wanted a meeting afterwards."

Kate swiveled toward her husband, "Ell, you told your brother-in-law a lie?"

"It wasn't a lie," he explained, "You told me we all needed to talk. I just reconfigured it to a meeting after dinner."

"You little fabricator," Kate wagged her index finger at her husband, "I'm going to have to keep an eye on you. Who's been rubbing off on you, huh?"

"I'll never tell." He reached over, enclosed her hand with his and kissed the finger she had been accusing him with.

"Oh," Kate's breath rushed out and she blushed, her heart pounding in her chest. She has known Ell since she was nineteen and he still had the power to take her breath away.

"Somebody get a bucket of cold water and cool these two down." Sam's voice broke through the fog in Kate's mind, and then she turned red as the words sank in.

"Cut it out, Sam," Anne teasingly scolded her younger sister. "It's nice to know there's still romance at *her age*." Anne and Sam both cracked up laughing.

Todd, Keith and even Ell slowly exited the dining room and hid in the kitchen, staying well out of the range of fire. They had learned early in their marriages that certain subjects only the sisters could tease about and get away with it.

Since Ell's two heart attacks and Kate's forced early retirement, she has been touchy about getting older. Her sister's never know when they can get away with an age wisecrack so they just take their chances and hope she doesn't blow up. This was *not* one of those times; the murder already had her on edge. Kate turned to her verbal attackers. No longer red faced with embarrassment but flushed with anger, and eyes normally a moss green was now a deep forest green. Her sister's quieted down quickly when they noticed she wasn't joining them in laughter.

"Well Anne, even though you are only three years younger, you haven't aged well with the strain from climbing that corporate ladder, and Sam, you're not doing very well in hiding those wrinkles you incurred as a result of bad decisions made in life either." Kate's voice was a tone lower than normal but the husbands still heard everything clearly. "Don't you think you both need to learn to accept others as they are, especially since you are no better in that category?"

Her sisters both had gone completely silent, their eyes wide with surprise. Mother and father had come out of their room to head down to the beach and stopped short when they got to the dining room table and heard Kate's dress down of her sisters. Before Anne and Sam could reply, mother stepped forward and whispered so that only the girls could hear. "Drop it right now, or so help me I will tell your husbands how much money you three spent when we went shopping the other day." Three shocked faces turned toward her. Its very seldom mother plays *that* trump card.

Sam was the first to recover and demurely replied, "Yes mother, sorry."

Anne first looked toward Kate as though it was her fault mother had to step in. "Sorry mother," she finally stated then hung her head as if she were still in grade school.

Kate audibly sucked in air and released it before she replied, "Sorry we upset you and dad. Everything is fine; we'll be okay now. Go ahead and have a nice walk." Kate finally gave her mother a weak smile.

"That's better, now give me a hug." Mother was smiling again, her arms outstretched and waiting. By the time the girls had each given their mother a hug, which was a requirement for the anger defusing, they were in a better frame of mind. This little incident would be forgotten in no time. After all, life was too short to stay angry, doing so shifts your priorities, festers into something ugly and in the end only changes you.

CHAPTER 7

▼

Keith, Todd and Ell finally sat down at the table. The girls had scattered after cleaning up the dinner dishes and still hadn't come back for the impromptu meeting. "Ell, you are not going to believe what we did while we were watching the coroner process the body." Todd had leaned toward Ell, who had sat across the table from him, and was talking in a conspirators' voice, looking over his shoulder before he continued. "You remember earlier when Keith was talking on the phone with his work?"

Ell nodded, he remembered Keith walking around in the family room talking on the phone while he and Kate had been setting things out in preparation for dinner, but he had not heard anything Keith had said. He had figured it was work related the way Keith had been pacing.

"Well, Keith automatically put the phone in his pocket without thinking and headed back out on the deck while we were watching dolphins. He remembered it was there after the sheriff left with the girls to talk to dad, so we took some pictures. We took a lot of pictures as a matter of fact," Todd replied excitedly. "We need to email them somewhere so we can print them off or maybe there is a tech store we can run them through. Do you know of any close by?"

Ell was stunned. They had pictures. Kate had wanted pictures and now they had them, she would be ecstatic. "Let's hope we don't have to go up to Wilmington. Kate's been trying to get me to take her to that slave museum again and I just got her off the subject until next year. Surely we can find one closer, maybe Calabash, they have begun to grow pretty fast, let's check there and Shallotte first. I'd even rather try Myrtle or North Myrtle beaches in South Carolina before tempting her with heading north to Wilmington; I just don't think she can handle it this year."

"Okay, we get it, exhaust all other avenues before Wilmington is even considered," Todd answered. "Where are those girls, we need to get this show on the road, so to speak."

☙

The girls were setting in Kate's room having a discussion of their own. A Sisters' talk long past due. They hadn't had a girl talk since the last Sisters' Weekend ten months ago. Stress from the murder had them all on edge and was causing them to react harshly when it was not needed. They wanted a few minutes together to straighten up loose ends before tackling what evidence they had gathered so far on this murder.

"First of all, I would like to apologize for my blow-up earlier," Kate began. "It was uncalled for and the only excuse I can give is stress. Please forgive me. I truly am sorry mother over heard; we usually clear things up before she knows anything. It was unfortunate they arrived in the room when they did."

"Of course we forgive you," Sam spoke first. "We both know your forced retirement was unforeseen, as was Ell's heart attacks."

"You know we love you no matter what," Anne offered, "Even when you make nasty mean remarks." She was still smarting because Kate's words had been truthful, and Grandma had always said the sting of truth was the worst.

"Sister's hug," Sam announced with her arms open wide.

Chapter 8

"It's about time," Todd told the girls as they came down the steps. "We thought you wanted to hear all the gruesome details?"

"First things first," Kate replied. "You never gloss over an argument and expect it to be okay. Sisters have an obligation to each other, not to mention the whole family to keep on good terms. So what have you got?"

"Keith took pictures," Ell began.

"Holy spa-moly!" Kate replied before Ell could finish. "It's just what we needed."

"Let me finish," Ell cut her off the tangent he was sure to come of what she felt was necessary information and documentation for any investigation. "I said he took pictures. They are still on his cell phone, we need a way to print them off because there is no way we can examine every detail in that tiny cell phone."

"Oh, so we need an Internet Café where we can hook-up and download onto a flash drive or memory stick and then, oh that's going to take too long. We need one of those geek stores where we can just take it in and they'll print them off for us." Kate had taken the ball and ran with it, as always, "Do we have one of those places anywhere close?"

"That's what we've been discussing while you ladies were upstairs," Ell informed her. "We think the closest place is in Myrtle Beach, we'll go first thing in the morning."

"I don't think we should leave mom and dad here by themselves all day while we go gallivanting along the coast," Sam informed the group.

"Maybe they would like to go out on the casino boat at Little River," Anne suggested. "We could drop them off on our way down and pick them up on the way back. They had wanted to check out a casino and that one could work to our advantage."

"That's an excellent idea Anne," Keith congratulated his wife, "And quick thinking."

"Thanks," Anne replied. "Mom mentioned it a few weeks ago when we were talking on the phone."

"Well, that just leaves talking to your parents when they get back," Todd finally spoke up. "Think they'll go for it?"

"Go for what?" Mother asked.

All eyes at the table turned toward their parents. They had been so engrossed in their discussion they hadn't heard them come in the door.

Mother repeated her question before she received an answer.

"Oh sorry, we didn't expect you quite so soon." Sam cleared her throat before continuing. "We planned on going into Myrtle Beach to get some pictures printed off Keith's camera and thought you might prefer waiting for us at the casino in Little River."

"And why would we prefer to wait for you there?" Mother had her hands on her hips waiting for an answer to satisfy why they didn't want her and her husband with them.

"Because the pictures are of the crime scene and we didn't think you would want to be involved in it." Kate stated matter-of-factly.

Mothers' hands slid down off her hips and her bristly manner smoothed back down. "You are absolutely correct. Drop us off at the casino." She added fathers jacket to hers hanging over her arm and headed toward the bedroom, "Jack dear, pour us some cranberry juice, will you? I am totally parched." Turning to the kids she asked, "When do we leave?"

"We don't want to be gone all day, so we figured we would need to get you to the casino before launch time, they still go out on four hour trips. We can drop you off early enough that we'll get to the mall at opening time and still be back to pick you up before the boat docks on it's return. We'll wait for you at the buffet and have lunch before we head back here. Does that sound okay?"

"I would think so." Mother was quiet a moment before she asked, "What does one wear to a casino?"

Kate laughed before she answered, "Whatever you want mom, it's not like the one in London where they dress to the nines."

"Oh." Mother replied then asked, "How much money do you take?"

"In my case," Sam answered, "Only as much as you want to lose."

"But aren't you supposed to win?"

"Very few do mom," Anne replied sadly.

"Then why bother?" Mother asked.

"For the fun and excitement," Kate answered. "Don't worry, you'll enjoy yourselves."

"I hope so. It sounds rather doubtful though if all we're going to do is lose money." Mother wasn't sure she still wanted to go, but decided it would be better than looking at pictures of some dead guy lying in the sand. The things you do for your kids. She and father took their glasses of juice and went to their room; if they were leaving that early they had better get some rest.

Chapter 9

Everyone except Blue was on the road bright and early the next morning. The inside door to the deck was left open to allow Blue a full view of the dunes for entertainment.

The Sphynx cats' ears are designed slightly different than other cats and due to the size and shape, their hearing is heightened to the point that they can hear electrical current on the airwaves. This is both good and bad for a cat, good because they miss nothing and bad because they hear everything. Usually they filter out normal sounds so they don't interfere with any new sound they are investigating, but it also makes them vulnerable to danger. Sphynx cats should never be allowed loose outside, which is why Blue gets stuck with a harness and leash when they travel. At home he has a maze of screened tunnels that are attached to the large screened gazebo his people enjoy spending time in.

Nearby he heard baby birds in a nest crying for food, and then the tone changed when a parent returned to feed them. Quickly his attention moved on to a scurrying sound below the decking in the sand and seconds later an anole pops up over the edge of a board searching for the best place to sun, or maybe looking for a juicy insect, Blue couldn't tell. Anole lizards' were very common on the island and looked similar to chameleons. Its quick jerky movements had his lips twitching with excitement while thoughts of catching such a tasty morsel raced through his head, but all too soon the anole slipped back down between the boards and out of sight. *Such was life,* Blue thought as he leaned his head against the glass to gaze down where the lizard had disappeared, *always in a hurry.*

Blue closed off the oceans' constant roar as he gazed across the deck. A new sound caused him to involuntarily tilt his head to one side to listen; the rhythmic footfalls of an animal in the sand below deck, they slowed then faded out completely. Blue wasn't sure what was under the deck, he had not been allowed anywhere but down the wooden walk and out to the soft sand that gathered along the base of the dune and that had been on the leash. People were not allowed to walk in the sea oats that were planted on the dunes to keep erosion at bay, but he had noticed cat prints along those rows. The salty wind had removed any lingering odors left behind in the loose sand but the cat had been confident enough with its' own area that it hadn't bothered to leave any other scent markings, so he had no idea if it was male or female.

Blue quickly became bored of just the sound of birds mixed with the ocean surf and scrunched down on his haunches to rest. His eyes were closed, although he was not asleep, he preferred to sleep on his peoples' bed in one of those soft fleece blankets.

The tantalizing odor of a female was slowly bringing Blue to full consciousness from a deeper dozing level than he had anticipated. Opening his eyes to a saucy little brown tabby with green eyes boldly starring back at him, Blue pulled back and hissed. The female didn't flinch and Blue was intrigued. He stepped up to the glass to look at her more closely. She titled her head to one side as though she were trying to figure out if he truly was a cat. Blue stretched up on his long legs and struck the pose that had won him *Best of Show* at nearly every exhibition he had attended.

The female stood up and walked from one side of the door to the other to examine Blue through the glass. He was like nothing she had ever seen before, and although Sphynx are no longer rare, they are not abundant either. The Sphynx breeders association keeps a tight reign on their catteries; the cost of a kitten will only drop if you have abundance on the market. Blue enjoyed showing off his form, with no hair to hide his muscular body, all was in plain view. He whipped his tail from side to side in a most masterful way. His lean fine boned body, triangular head, tall ears and slightly slanted green eyes were magnificent. Blue was glad he hadn't had time to get dirty yet, his blue hair, only the length of peach fuzz, literally glowed a pale blue in the sunlight.

The female must have been impressed; she walked up and bumped the top of her head on the door, and then slowly tilted her head to the side and rubbed the length of her body across the glass door. Blue opened his mouth in a grimace hoping to catch her scent. She had chosen him and he would find a way to get out of the house. The pull of nature was a strong beast and one he didn't intend to fight.

Blue jumped up and hung on the door latch but it was locked and he dropped back down to rethink his escape. Staring intently at the thumb latch, he turned his head first one way and then the other, trying to figure out how to get it unlocked.

His saucy female was giving him encouraging little mews and pawing the glass. Finally she walked over to the attached deck bench and jumped up to wait, watching his every move.

Blue jumped up again and braced his hind feet on the glass as his front feet clung to the handle. He studied it and wiggled it, and then studied it some more. The handle had a small lever that fit into a rectangular cut opening. If he could pull the lever back out, he would be able to open the door, but it would not move with his weight on the handle. He dropped back down to the floor and stretched his long legs up to the latch. He could feel the curve of the metal under his soft pad, but it needed quite a bit of persuasion before he was able to get it to move. Once the lever was removed from the plate on the handle, Blue was able to jump up, pull down on the handle and push off on the door casing to be free. The feeling was exhilarating and had him a little light headed. The door hushed back and latched itself with only a light scratch on the door casing to show his escape.

The little female jumped off the bench and ran to him. Now it was her turn to stand and let him inspect her physique. Blue was impressed with her equally fine boned structure; he was smitten immediately, she was true beauty in his eyes. Finally, they headed out to the gazebo and on down the steps to search out new adventures together.

Being this was the first time Blue had ever been outside without supervision, he wasn't sure how long it would last, but he intended to make the most of it, knowing all too soon his people would be on his trail.

Chapter 10

"Dad, try to keep mom occupied, if she doesn't hit on a machine after a couple of spins move her on to another one, you don't want to lose everything in one machine." Anne, the business minded, was instructing father while Samantha and Kate talked to mother.

"Mom, remember you have to put in the maximum amount of coins to get the big money or the jackpot if it comes up. Your best bet is to hit the Max Bet button, that way you know you have the full amount needed to win the maximum payout." Kate hoped mother understood what they were trying to explain, because she looked totally confused.

"Of course, it eats up your money a lot quicker that way too," Sam began. "If you only want to play one coin, I suggest you play the two coin slot machines, the payout is higher than playing one coin in the three coin machines."

Mothers' eyes seemed to be telling them she wasn't sure this was a good idea, but never once did she speak. Her head bobbed up and down as Sam and Kate tried to explain how the machines worked but she knew her best bet, would be to watch other people play before trying it herself.

All too soon the girls were shooing them through the gateway and waving them goodbye.

"I feel like I've been given the bum's rush, don't you?" Mother stood beside her husband as they watched their daughters scurry out of sight.

"You knew they wanted to be at that store when it opened," Father answered.

"I know," she sighed, "it's just we see so little of them nowadays. I think we would have enjoyed coming to the casino more if everyone was going to be here with us." She slowly turned around, and then headed toward the crowd that was milling around a buffet table with an unusual array of edible flowers not to mention regular breakfast items, she needed a hot cup of her Chinese tea but coffee would just have to do.

CR

The girls finally got mother and father onto the boat and headed back out to Kate's van. "Do you think they'll have a good time?" Anne was worried her plan to drop them off would flop and their parents' first casino experience would be a bad one. Anne got into the van beside her husband in the second bench seat. "Hey, this is real comfortable when you're not squeezed in."

"Middle aged spread wouldn't have anything to do with being squeezed in would it?" Sam quipped as she joined her husband in the first bench seat.

"Hey ..." Anne began.

Kate didn't let Anne finish, "What did we discuss last night?" Kate tried not to sound like mother scolding them, but failed miserably.

"I was only teasing, we've all gained weight," Sam admitted.

"I know and personally I don't want to dwell on my weight gain while I'm on vacation thank you," Kate informed them. "So let's concentrate on this murder right now shall we?"

"You're such a potty poopa," Sam tried to imitate Arnold from the movie he had said the line in and had everyone in the van laughing, and so set the mood for the rest of the trip to Myrtle Beach.

Chapter 11

Sitting on the corner of the out-lot strip that surrounded Myrtle Beach Mall sat the building they were looking for. Evidently, technical support is *the* thing to be knowledgeable in. The inside of the store was nothing they had expected; while there were several work stations located around the store, most of the workers, all under the age of thirty and male, were already busy helping phone customers or preparing to go out on support runs. It was a virtual hub of activity.

"Holy mackerel," Samantha exclaimed, "it's like a bee hive in here."

"What do you suppose they'll charge for this download and print?" Keith feared the cost after seeing some of the most expensive computer systems he had ever seen in his life sitting in this very room.

"What does it matter, we still have to have it done," Todd replied. "Besides, we already agreed to divide up the cost."

After what only seemed seconds due to they're gawking in awe at the equipment and activity, a gentleman appeared at their side. "My name is Aaron, may I help you?"

"Oh!" Kate lifted only slightly off the ground at his voice. She had been so absorbed in all the work going on he had caught her unaware and her heart was pounding. While she calmed her breathing down with Ell at her side, Keith explained their situation.

"We're on vacation and we've taken some pictures with my phone that we want to download onto a compact disc or even a memory stick plus we want printouts of the pictures." Keith figured if this bunch couldn't get it done then they were up a creek.

"No problem," Aaron replied. "How many photo copies do you need?"

Not knowing what the cost would be Keith told him one set and Aaron headed over to one of the workstations. Sitting down he punched a few numbers on the phone, and then handed it back to Keith. "It will only take a few minutes to register. Are you enjoying your vacation?" His eyebrows slipped under his hairline when they all burst out laughing. "Did I miss something; you did say you were on vacation didn't you?"

"We don't mean to be rude," Ell was the first to get control of his laughter. "When you see the photos you'll understand our reaction to your question."

The machine behind Aaron beeped and he turned around to open the email. "Whoa that is gross, is that … yeah it is … where did you take these … oh man these are gruesome … I've got to show these to the guys."

The small group was overtaken by nearly every employee in the store, huddling close to get a look at the photos. The sister's group stepped back to allow the others in for a closer look. Obviously, this was the most excitement this store has had in awhile. Eventually Aaron shooed them back to work and turned to face Keith. "Why do you have these photos?"

"We're staying next door to the crime scene and my father-in-law witnessed the discovery of the body," Keith answered. "What do we owe you?"

"The pictures are $12.50 and the memory stick is $18.95, will that be cash or charge?" Aaron handed Anne the package.

"Cash is fine, thank you. Don't forget to delete that email, we plan on giving the memory stick to the sheriff." Keith paid the bill and they exited through the door they had entered earlier.

Once they were back in the parking lot Anne wanted to see the photos. "Is there some place close we can all sit down and get a look at these before heading back to meet mom and dad?"

"We're going to need a table large enough to spread out all these pictures," Sam's mind was already at work. "What about that pancake restaurant over there?"

"Can't we just sit on a picnic table at one of those putt-putt joints that hasn't opened for the day back on the strip?" Kate was trying to keep Ell and her from eating again so soon, neither of them needed anything heavy as a midmorning snack.

"Let's hope the cops don't arrest us for loitering and take our photos before we get to see them," Ell was just as anxious to see them as everyone else, and he would hate to lose them before he could give them a good study.

"Fine, but if I gain anymore weight I refuse to be seen in my swimsuit on the beach." Kate knew when to give in; some arguments aren't worth the trouble. Everyone climbed back into the van and they drove over to the restaurant.

CR

They passed the pictures around between bites of the Belgium waffles they hadn't been able to resist. "Okay, who got the blueberry stain on the picture?" Kate complained; she had nearly done the same thing with her strawberries.

"Sorry, that was me, I got carried away with my serving size when I found out they had made the syrup with fresh blueberries." Samantha had lost a blueberry off her forkful of waffle and it had not only dropped onto the photo but had rolled across the picture before it stopped. The carnage left in its wake was brutal, and although Sam had done her best to clean it, the stain was there to stay.

"The guy looks like he has a blue scar across his chest," Ell stated when he saw the photo they had been discussing. "Sort of like a Frankenstein stitch job, I hope I never get one like that."

"Ell stop it, you know I don't like you joking about going into surgery." Kate wasn't in any rush to go in that direction just yet. Ell had been lucky enough to only need a catheter to insert the stainless steel stints after his heart attacks, and if he watched his lifestyle he wouldn't have any other problems.

"Whoa, you guys did a good job with the pictures," Anne jumped in to get everyone's attention back on the subject. "How did you get so many without the coroner seeing you?"

"I blocked their view, mainly I kept their eyes on me while Keith took the pictures," Todd answered her. "It was easy, Keith stayed pretty much in the same place while I moved first one way then another. They were so worried I was going to get in the way they didn't see Keith taking the pictures, and of course I kept up a non-stop flow of questions."

"Well, you two work great together, these are good shots." Anne moved her photos on to Keith before taking another syrupy bite.

"You girls should have seen Todd, he was flitting around from person to person like a bee, and some of his questions were pretty technical," Keith told them.

Todd shrugged his shoulder, "I watch a lot of CSI, doesn't everyone?"

They all laughed in agreement. Finally they relaxed and began to chit chat about the turn of events during their vacation as they finished up their waffles. All too soon they needed to get back on the road to pick up mother and father on time. Hopefully, their parents had enjoyed themselves today in their new experience.

Chapter 12

▼

Dexie came out of the galley absolutely glowing, the prized recipe grasped in her hand. She couldn't wait to make it for the kids, Blue Flower Chive Omelet; she knew they would just love it. She and Jack had sampled it on the breakfast buffet as the boat had headed out to international waters. After finding the chef she hounded him until he finally gave in, but the cost was a trade for Kate's risotto recipe. The boat had already turned back toward shore before she began her search to find her husband. She hoped he had found something to keep him entertained. Earlier she had shooed him out to the gaming floor once she realized getting the recipe was going to take a little more time than she expected.

Dexie waded through the crowds at the slot machines, but didn't find Jack. She headed to the roulette tables, but once again found no husband. Turning toward the poker room she caught sight of him at one of the tables, cards in hand and several stacks of chips setting in front of him. Rather than disturb his concentration she stood in the back to watch until the hand was finished. Glancing around the room, most of the people were sitting and playing, but there were quite a few watching too.

One woman in particular caught her eye. She had short snow-white hair with soft curls on top that blended down to a light wave just at the bottom of her earlobes. She was dressed casual but the clothes were high end. Her tan was obviously from a booth this early in the season. The hackles on the back of Dexie's neck began to rise. This woman had no business standing so close to her husband. Jealousy began to rear its ugly head and she had to take a deep breath to get it under control.

Dexie made her way around the room along the back wall to get a look from a different angle. Perhaps she was mistaken and the woman was with someone else and just happened to be standing behind her husband. It was definitely crowded around that particular table.

Finally taking the plunge, she headed straight toward the table. Her husband had laid his cards down face up and the crowd standing around the table began to clap. Jack was pulling the pile of chips in the middle of the table toward him when Dexie reached his side.

"Hello dear, you look pretty pleased with yourself," Dexie purred as she bent next to her husband.

"Very pleased," he replied to Dexie without looking at her and then he announced to the table he was finished for the day. The gaming attendant quickly handed him cups to put the chips in and escorted him to the nearest cashier. Jack handed the attendant some chips once the cups were set on the counter. The attendant thanked him before he headed back to the poker room to help clear off the tables as prevention to keep the gamblers from starting up a game while they were still docked.

While the cashier dumped and counted the chips, Dexie presented the question to Jack that had been causing her stomach to churn. "So who was that attractive woman standing next to you?"

"Attractive woman ... oh I know who you mean," Jack began, "Turns out she lives down the beach from where we're staying. She recognized me and came up to introduce herself."

"I bet she did," Dexie whispered under her breath.

"How would you like that sir?" The cashier asked, interrupting their conversation.

"Hundreds will be fine," was his reply before he turned back toward his wife's question.

"Hundreds?" Dexie had raised one eyebrow.

Jack smiled then raised one shoulder and informed her, "I wasn't as rusty as I thought."

☙

Heading back across the boat to prepare for debarking, the same woman that was in the poker room once again approached them. Extending her hand to shake, she introduced herself. "Vera Johnson, I live a few houses down from Tiwardrai. Quite an appalling discovery wasn't it? The body I mean."

The woman was obviously a talker. She barely gave them time to introduce themselves, not that they had planned on elaborating. Dexie already had her opinion of the woman set in her mind, and Jack was barely listening, he didn't want to get caught in the crush when they left the boat and was keeping an eye out for the best route off.

"I haven't seen that much excitement on the island the entire forty years I've lived there." It appeared Vera had an audience and she wasn't about to let them go. She walked with them all the way to the front exit and stood waiting with them for the boat to pull up and dock. She explained how the beach had changed, how it used to be all land owners living there and now nearly everyone rents their beach houses most of the year. People don't respect the properties or the beach and erosion was breaking down the dunes.

Dexie and Jack only nodded or mumbled single replies as she droned on. Vera didn't seem to notice it was a one-sided conversation; obviously she lived alone and needed someone to talk to, Dexie thought as she glanced over at the woman. Finally, the boat was docked and they began letting everyone off. Dexie pointed out to Jack where the children were waiting for them and then turned to Vera, "It was nice to meet you," she stated not waiting for Vera to respond. Grabbing her husband's arm she literally dragged him through the throng of people to get to her awaiting children. It felt like she had been away from her girls for days instead of hours.

Chapter 13

"Mom, did you have a good time?" Anne still felt bad about dumping them at the casino alone. "You didn't get lost from dad did you?"

"I am perfectly capable of finding him if I did thank you." Mother continued with, "I'm not senile you know."

"I didn't mean that," Anne said.

"I know dear, and we did have a good time, we'll tell you about it later. How did things work out for you kids?" Mother linked her arm with Anne's as they headed toward the van.

"Oh splendid," Anne replied, "just splendid."

"So Dad, did Mom leave all her money on the boat?" Sam and Kate had linked their arms with their father to get his version and they would corner Mom and get hers later.

"As far as I know she didn't spend any money. Truth be told, I didn't see her play at all," he replied.

"Oh dad, was it that awful?" Kate was now feeling bad that they had left them by themselves.

"No, I think we both had a good time, we just weren't together," he stated.

"Oh no, Mom didn't get lost did she?" Sam couldn't believe it.

"Not lost per say but I better let your mother explain," Father answered, "I don't seem to be doing a very good job of it. So, how was your trip? Everything work out for you?"

"It did," Sam replied. "We got photos and had the guys copy it onto a memory stick for the police. Some of the pictures are really gross dad."

"Death is never pretty when its' murder, you just keep that in mind, both of you." He squeezed their arms closer as they finally arrived at the vehicle. Keith had gotten out of the front passenger seat to let Kate get in and he climbed in the back next to his wife.

"Seat belts on?" Ell turned and smiled to everyone.

"Do we have to? We're packed in here like sardines now." Todd hated the thought of fighting with the belt.

"I'll tell you what Todd, if we get stopped and you cause us to get a seatbelt violation, you can pay the ticket, how's that sound?" Ell was still smiling, he knew Todd would cave.

"Okay," Todd relented, "but I'm doing so under protest."

"Duly noted, I wouldn't have expected anything less." Ell turned back around and put the van in gear, "anyone hungry?"

Kate gave Ell a playful punch on his upper arm, "How can you think of food so soon, are you a bottomless pit?"

"No, I thought maybe your mom or dad might be hungry," he replied softly.

"Oh, sorry" Kate turned toward her parents in the middle seat, "are you two hungry, we can stop on the way home if you want?"

"No, I think we can wait till we get back to the beach house," her mother answered, "but thanks for asking."

"We planned on stopping at the sheriff's office to drop off a copy of the pictures," Ell was looking at them in the rear view mirror as he talked. "It'll probably take an extra fifteen minutes, is that okay?"

"We'll be fine," father answered. "We had a nice big breakfast on the boat, didn't we dear?"

"Yes we did." Mother smiled as she thought of her new recipe hiding in her pocket. "Oh by the way Kate, I'm going to need another copy of your risotto recipe; I seem to have misplaced mine."

"Mother I just gave that to you last night," Kate's eyebrows were raised a good inch higher then normal, "how could you lose it?"

"I had it in my purse and now it's gone, and no, I didn't lay it somewhere else." Mother appeared as if she were pouting as she added, "Could you just write out a new one please?"

"Very well," Kate answered, "but I'm going to be keeping an eye on you."

Ell pulled into a large parking lot that serviced several municipal offices including the Sheriff's and the County Jail. Keith and Todd got out of the vehicle to deliver the memory stick while the others waited in the van.

☙

Arriving at the beach house, Kate became quiet after they had gotten out of the van and headed up the walk toward the beach house. She had pin pricks on the back of her neck, something was wrong. The once beautiful walkway was now too long, her steps quickened to a near run. The closer they got to the house, the more apprehensive she became. Her chest tightened to almost unbearable pain, and her fears hit her square in the face as she pushed open the door. It was Blue.

Chapter 14

Kate and Ell had been to every house on the island with no luck. They did leave a few notes on doors but other than that, no one had seen Blue. Anne and Keith had walked the beach waterline and Sam and Todd had followed the tracks on the dunes until they disappeared. Mother and Father had stayed at the house and prepared sandwiches and a fresh fruit salad for when they would return.

Sam and Todd were back first, the tracks were really only indentations and could have been made by any small animal. They strangely went down to the area of the beach where the dead body had been before they returned to the top of the dune and continued. A third set of tracks crossed the two sets on top of the dune before it headed out onto the sidewalk. That set never returned to the sand. Sam hoped he was not stolen. They had not found any blood to show he was injured and they did not find a body, but that was a small relief.

Anne and Keith came in off the deck. They had been dreading coming in, the only ray of hope they had to share was they hadn't found his lifeless body on the beach, and that was small consolation for losing a loved one.

"Why don't you get something to eat," mother told each of them as they arrived, "it's going to be a long day if Kate and Ell come back without Blue."

"How could this have happened? He's been here all week and hasn't messed with the door lock." Sam was baffled, "why would he experiment now?"

"Who knows, cats are strange creatures," Anne returned. "Why do they do any of the crackpot things they do?"

"Point taken," Sam replied.

By late afternoon, Todd and Keith informed their wives they were going upstairs to the gallery for a while, in case they would be needed. Sam and Anne noticed they took the envelope of pictures with them. A lost cat wasn't enough to hold their attention like a murder and they both had done all they could to help, so the girls let them go without an argument while they stayed downstairs with mother and father waiting on Kate and Ell's return.

Afternoon turned into evening and still they had not returned. Mother and father were beginning to worry when they heard their arrival. Kate was sobbing uncontrollably as they entered the front hall. Mother was afraid they had found him dead and came rushing over to them. Ell shook his head at mother's questioning eyebrow.

Todd and Keith popped their heads over the upper railing of the gallery. Anne shook her head to let them know he wasn't found and they returned to the job they had taken upon themselves to do, organizing the photos.

"I'm going to put her to bed, and then I'll be back down," Ell told them. "Did any of you bring a mild sedative with you? She needs rest desperately."

"All I have are muscle relaxants and I don't know if you want her to take those," Sam offered.

"I have some," Anne whispered, "take her on up and I'll get them."

"Thanks Anne," Ell replied softly.

Kate would have gladly collapsed on the stairs had it not been for Ell and her father. They managed to get her in the room and on the bed before another fit of sobbing broke loose. Father got the box of tissues and Ell opened a bottle of water she kept on the side table as Anne arrived with the pill. Getting the pill down Kate was a fight but eventually accomplished, father and Anne went back downstairs while Ell held her until she fell asleep.

›¿

When Ell returned downstairs, the strain on his face worried the rest of the family. He didn't need this stress on his heart. Mother handed him a tall glass of grape juice and asked if he would like a turkey sandwich. He told her yes and she brought it back to the dining room table with a bowl of fruit salad, a napkin and a fork. He drank half of his glass of juice before he began to talk.

"We went to every house on the island and no one has seen him. How could he have not been seen by anyone? We left notes on several houses but I think a lot of those were empty this week." Ell massaged his temples as he stated. "I don't know what else we can to do."

"You need to rest," Mother began. "He is probably scared and hiding somewhere, we'll find him. At least we didn't find him dead, that's a good sign. Now, finish your sandwich and go on up and rest while Kate is, she's going to need your strength when she wakes up."

Ell finished his meal and forced down his evening pills before heading back up to the bedroom. He hadn't realized he cared so much for the little cat. Silently he whispered a prayer promising never to complain about Blue's ritual of rooting under the covers for the perfect spot in bed every night, if they got him back.

Chapter 15

Mother and father had been up for a couple of hours when the phone rang at eight that morning, it was Sheriff Poole and she handed the phone to her husband. He listened for a few seconds before answering.

"You know my feelings on our paying for extended accommodations. We did nothing wrong, so we shouldn't have to pay just because *you* feel we might need to be questioned again. Come out this morning with your questions before we leave or pay for us to stay until you do come out," he said into the phone.

The sheriff talked for quite a while before Jack answered him. "I don't care, this is clearly harassment of law abiding citizens, either you pay or we leave, it's that simple." Without saying goodbye he pushed the end button and set the phone back in it's holder for recharging, fully expecting the phone to ring before he got back to the table and his conversation with his wife.

"Jack, you know we can't leave until we find Blue, it would kill Kate." Dexie handed her husband his cup of coffee she had just topped off.

"He doesn't have to know that, and besides, we've got a few hours before we have to leave, he could show up before then." Jack was being optimistic; knowing the possibility of the cat doing just that would be a long shot.

Mother raised her eyes above her husband's head to watch Keith and Todd come down the stairs with their wives a few steps behind them. They all looked as though they hadn't slept much, understandably so in this situation. "Try to eat the cereal so we don't have to take it back home with us," she told them as they gravitated toward the kitchen past her and father sitting at the dining room table. "I started a new pot of coffee so give it a few minutes."

"Who was on the phone a few moments ago?" Anne asked as she poured two bowls of raisin bran flakes.

"That was the sheriff trying to force us into delaying our departure date," father replied.

"But dad, we can't leave until we find Blue." Anne was astonished her father would even consider the notion of doing so.

"I know that, but the sheriff doesn't have to know it. We're not going anywhere until that little scoot is found," he informed her.

"What does it matter that the sheriff knows it or not," Sam asked.

"If Blue shows up before we leave, we won't have to pay to spend another night, and we'll just leave a few hours later than normal." Father continued, "We will make the decision later in the day if we need to stay another night. We can stay at the motel here on the island a night at a time if necessary. It's none of the sheriff's business."

"Dad, you're making things more difficult than they need to be. We stay for Blue or we stay for the sheriff, it's no different we'll stay either way," Anne stated.

"It's the principal honey, one is choice and one is not," father said.

The phone rang as Anne opened her mouth to reply. Grabbing the annoying noise maker off it's charger she spoke a little more gruffly than expected. "Hello!"

"Oh, sorry," Anne said waiting a few seconds before continuing, "Sure, hang on a moment." Stretching her arm out into the air she stated, "Dad, it's for you, Sheriff Poole," then she smiled when he made a grimace before taking the phone from her. Sometimes life has its own agenda and takes the reigns right out of your hands.

Father spoke few words and the furrow growing between his eyes indicated he was not happy with this particular telephone call. He walked back and forth in front of the counter before finally replacing the handset in its cradle only slightly harder than need be.

"Impudent pup," he stated as he walked back to the table and sat down. "It appears we will be staying here a few days longer than expected. The sheriff took it upon himself to contact the owners of this beach house and arrange it, at no cost to ourselves except our time. If you need to contact your workplace I suggest you get it done, who knows how long they will want us to stay," he stated and then added, "surely not more than a week."

"Dad, I don't know if Todd can get extra time off," Sam spoke as Todd cleared away their breakfast dishes and refilled Sam and his coffee cups.

"I'll call HR and give him the situation," Todd told her. "I don't think there will be a problem, they can call the temp agency."

Keith was already talking to the Vice President at Anne and his work, but he had run into a snag. The person covering his job this week was leaving tomorrow for a ten day cruise and they weren't sure just who could fill in until Keith returned.

Anne overheard his conversation and rolled her eyes before taking the cell phone from him. "Ted, Larry should be able to handle both his and Keith's offices. No, we knew these few weeks were going to be thin on personnel so we pushed appointments to later in the month. I know, but the only thing he will have to worry about is walk-ins, he can order in his lunch and take the extra time off when we get back. Oh, and let Jesse know he'll have to do the payroll since I won't be there. Yes, he's done it before. Thanks Ted and give our regards to Prudence. We'll call as soon as we get back home." Anne pushed the end button and handed the phone back to Keith, he was smiling, obviously amused with her bossiness to the vice president. Anne was pleased herself, she had worked hard to get to the position she was in, knowing what every office did and who could run it was immense value. It made her *the person to see* when there was a problem at the company. By all appearances, she thrived on that kind of power.

CHAPTER 16

▼

The wind whisked away the sharp edges of their footprints as Blue followed Nellie across the hot sand dunes. The skin on his back was beginning to tingle; he hoped he wasn't getting a sun burn. The female cat was headed for her home ground, only a few houses down from where Blue was staying. They went into the house through the pet door on the back deck. Blue was mesmerized with Nellie, she was quite an intelligent female and very opinionated.

They had chatted a lot as they walked, their paws sunk deep into the sand leaving no definite shape. Blue had convinced Nellie to detour past the spot where the body was found before they continued on to her home. He figured it would be the only opportunity he'd have and he couldn't pass it up. She was only mildly curious and felt people were strange folks, always arguing and then leaving. Nellie had given up trying to make friends with any human other than her current caregiver.

Pushing through the pet door, Nellie gave Blue a tour of the house, taking him into her room last. Yes, she had a room of her own and it was like nothing he had ever seen before. Steps only eighteen inches wide ran up one wall and connected to a ledge the same depth running around the entire room. A ledge butted up to the windows facing the beach conveniently giving a cat the optimal view and allowed a generous amount of light into the room. Blue was impressed and in awe, the room had been specifically designed for a cat. At one time it had only been an ordinary bedroom he was sure, but now it was a cat's dream.

Being the hostess, Nellie offered Blue a bite of food from her touch of the paw self-feeder and a drink of water from her miniature water fountain. He pawed at the water several times as it sprayed into the air before getting a drink. They ran over to her jungle play area which took up three quarters of the room and nearly wore themselves out chasing each other in and out and up and down on the multi-level of tree limbs and carpet covered barrels before nature took over and things became more serious. When Blue woke hours later the windows indicated it was dark outside, he knew his human companions would be worried but he couldn't force himself to leave Nellie just yet.

He burrowed under the edge of the cover she was lying on to ward off the chill from the air conditioning and drifted into a sleep of contentment. Such was the life of pampered pets floated through his mind, he could get used to this kind of living really quick.

❦

Vera pulled off the note taped on her front door before unlocking and pushing it open. She hadn't planned on staying out this late, but she had met someone that could be a possibility for her future. Flipping on the light she tossed her purse on the hall table and read the note as she walked toward the back door. *Lost Sphynx cat, REWARD!!!!* A phone number was listed, evidently a cell, she didn't recognize the area code.

Vera moaned audibly at someone's loss, she herself would be a mess if Nellie wasn't around to keep her company. Walking through the house she announced to her cat that mommy was home, she dropped the note on the kitchen counter before sliding the board into the slot on the pet door. She had awoken to feral cats running through the house before and she was too tired for it to happen tonight. Returning to the refrigerator she got out a cold bottle of water to set on her night stand. When Nellie didn't appear as she normally did Vera headed upstairs stopping by the little cat's room first to check and make sure she was indeed in the house. Without turning on the light she walked over and peeked into Nellie's basket. The moon barely lit the room but it was enough that Vera could see the familiar ball of fur. Smiling she turned and left the room ready for a good nights rest.

Chapter 17

It was nearly noon when Vera pulled herself out of bed and headed for the shower. She verbally chastised herself for wasting half the day in bed. She still had groceries to buy for the evening meal she was preparing for her new gentleman friend.

Half an hour later, Vera walked into the kitchen expecting to see Nellie lying sprawled across the floor in the warm sunshine, but she was not there. Vera called for her then turned and began beating eggs for a light lunch. Hearing the thump her cat made as she jumped the last three steps, Vera smiled as she glanced in that direction but was greeted with quite a surprise.

Nellie trotted across the living room toward the kitchen, but she was not alone. Vera had never personally seen a Sphynx cat before but when this cat trotted confidently into the room beside Nellie, it could not have been anything else. His regal ambiance exhibited him as an expensive breed and his hairless skin proved he was indeed a Sphynx. Setting her bowl of eggs aside she reached down and ruffled the fur behind Nellie's ears asking her who her friend was. Nellie gave up no secrets as she purred for her owner. Vera stood back up and reached for the note she had tossed on the counter at three o'clock this morning. This cat's owner would be near hysterics by now, she thought as she began to punch the numbers on the wall phone.

Chapter 18

Ell descended the stairs alone; it had been a rough night. Kate was finally in the shower, after Ell convinced her she was doing Blue no good by wallowing in pity. They needed to get back out there and keep looking, besides contacting the local animal shelter.

"How's she doing this morning?" Father was reading a newspaper he had picked up earlier, it was nearly ten. Mother, Anne and Samantha were in the kitchen taking stock of what was needed for the next few days. They were preparing for a grocery run. Keith and Todd were upstairs in the gallery of course, with everything they had that pertained to the murder, including news articles they had gotten this morning.

"I think she's numb, she hasn't talked much since waking up, but she will be down in a bit." Ell walked into the kitchen as the women were coming out. "Good morning."

Mother laid her hand on Ell's arm, "Be strong for her Ell, I'm sure we'll find him."

Ell patted her hand, "I hope so, although she did say he wasn't hurt."

"I'm sure she would feel it in her bones if he was. I'm glad he's not, so now all we have to do is find the little scoot," mother replied before walking on past him.

"Is there something we need to eat up before packing?" Ell asked, and then noticed there were no boxes waiting to be packed. "Did I miss something by staying in bed late?"

"The sheriff called this morning and informed us we were being detained," father answered. "*He* contacted the owners of the beach house and worked out a deal, at a reduced price I'm sure since it's being paid by the taxpayers. *We* won't be paying any money to stay, just our time, the others have already called back home and got it squared away. The sheriff hasn't said how long, we're hoping no more than a week. Is that going to cause a problem for you two?"

"I don't think so, but Kate would know for sure," Ell said as he poured a bowl of spoon sized frosted wheat. "She keeps a pocket calendar with her at all times. Besides, we wouldn't have left without Blue anyway, so I guess it's no big deal."

Ell walked over to the table and sat down just as Kate came into the room. "Honey, the sheriff called this morning and it looks like we're going to have to stay a bit longer, not that we would have left without Blue, but maybe a week they think."

"Yeah, whatever," Kate mumbled. No matter how much cold water she had splashed on her face, she still looked like something the cat dragged in, no pun intended. "Is there any creamer left? I'm going to need a whole pot of coffee to survive today."

"That coffee has been there a couple of hours," mother informed her. "Why don't you brew a fresh pot?"

"Yeah, whatever," Kate repeated her earlier reply.

Mother came over and stood in front of Kate, speaking for only her ears. "That will be enough self pity; you are not helping Blue acting like this. Now, get your breakfast down you and get back out there and look for him."

As Kate's eyes widened at her mother's sharp tongue, she knew she was right and it was nearly the same thing Ell had told her earlier. Giving her mother a hug she replied, "I'm sorry, you are right of course, he is expecting me to find him and he may not think he is lost."

"Oh, and if he'll let you, take your sisters with you and let Ell stay here and rest, he looks totally worn out. You know all that stress isn't good for him." Mother added in a whisper.

"I think I can do that," Kate whispered back. "Thanks mom."

The sisters had taken Anne's car and driven slowly. They stopped at the houses Kate and Ell had left notes at and either asked the person if they had seen Blue or removed the note. Only one house had removed the note but did not answer the door when they knocked, Kate figured she could return later. It was the last house they stopped at before heading home for lunch. Mother would have it ready by now, it was just after twelve.

Chapter 19

Lunch was on the table when they arrived back at the beach house. They couldn't have timed it any closer. The girls washed up in the kitchen sink and everyone sat down.

"Only one house left to check," Kate began. "If they haven't seen him then he's holed up somewhere probably scared to death. He's never been on his own before."

"What does your gut feeling tell you?" Mother handed the teriyaki penne salad to Anne before looking directly at Kate for her answer.

Kate closed her eyes to concentrate, "He's not hurt, or I would feel it. I'm getting a tranquil feeling or maybe it's a feeling of satisfaction ..." Kate's voice trailed off then her eyes popped open, "he's with a female! That little stinker, he had us worried to death!"

"I thought as much after checking out the door," mother said as all eyes turned her way. "While everyone was out looking for Blue, your father and I examined the door and deck boards. We found nose prints and cat hair stuck to the glass on the outside of the door.

Since there wasn't any blood on the deck, we figured it was a female looking for company and not a male out securing his territory."

"Well that's a fine how do you do," Kate exclaimed. "You could have told us!"

"You wouldn't have absorbed it in the state you were in," mother told her. "Besides, we weren't sure and I had hoped you would have relied on your instinct first instead of falling apart like you did. You disappointed me Kate. You need to distance yourself from the problem so you can grasp what your body is telling you."

They were interrupted by Kate and Ell's cell phone ringing. Ell stood up so fast he knocked over his chair. He was glad for that interruption, he knew where mother and Kate's discussion was headed and he wasn't in the mood for it right now. He pushed the button, "hello?"

"Yes, he's blue, or he may by now be gray due to rutting around in the dirt. He can't seem to keep clean. No he doesn't wear a collar because he nearly choked to death when he got it caught on the bottom scroll of our bakers rack." Ell was quiet a few moments before continuing, "We'll be over right away. Thank you." Pushing the end button he turned to tell everyone about Blue and found they had all left the table and were standing behind him. "The address is only a few houses west of here, Kate and I will go pick him up, you all finish lunch. Oh, and save some of that pasta for me for when I get back. It's got a nice kick to it, I like it."

"That's the fresh grated ginger in it," mother replied. "You two go on and get Blue; we'll be here when you get back."

"Let me get his blanket," Kate turned to go upstairs before continuing, "Who knows what condition he's in, he's probably filthy as usual."

Returning back downstairs Kate asked Ell if he had an extra hundred on him as they headed out the walk toward the van.

Ell almost came to a stop when he exclaimed, "You plan on paying a hundred dollars?"

"How much is he worth to you Ell?" Kate kept walking, in a rush to get to Blue.

"Enough said," Ell replied, then continued, "But it's going to put us in a pinch going home."

"Then we will make sandwiches to take with us or eat the two for a dollar hotdogs when we stop at the gas station along the way." Kate didn't miss a beat as she climbed in the van, she'd go without food if she had too, she could afford to lose a few pounds anyway.

◦≳

As Ell pulled in the drive to park, Kate noticed it was the same house she and her sisters had not gotten an answer to their knock. Kate was a little confused as to why this person wouldn't answer the door earlier. When the woman answered the door with damp hair Kate understood, this woman had been in the shower and simply had not heard their knock.

Ell spoke first, "We really appreciate your call, we were beginning to think he was gone forever and I don't think my wife would have recovered, she dotes on him so."

"I know how she feels," Vera replied. "Won't you come in? My name is Vera and yours is?"

"I'm Ellsworth and this is my wife Kate," Ell began. "We've been staying at Tiwardrai all week."

Kate noticed only the slightest tenseness in Vera's shoulders when Ell mentioned the name of the house they were staying at before it was gone. Taking a step forward Kate held her hand out to shake hands with Vera, she wanted to see if she could pick up any vibrations from this woman's tension.

Vera grasped Kate's hand and everything in the room turned red. Kate's ears began to ring and a collage of pictures flashed in her head, all were men and they too were red. As far as Kate could tell before Vera pulled back her hand, there were possibly nine different faces and Kate knew in her soul they were dead. The contact had only taken a few seconds to flood her senses and Kate needed to clear her mind to function properly. She closed her eyes to dispel the images.

"You must be Jack and Dexie's kids," Vera stated, unaware of the change in Kate's eyes when she reopened them. "I met them on the casino boat at Little River yesterday."

Ell jumped in when he noticed Kate collecting her thoughts, "Oh yes, dad did mention they had met someone from the island. Well, it's nice to meet you." He stretched his arm out to shake hands.

"Yes, they were having quite a day of it from what I could see," Vera volunteered, hoping to get a little more information from them.

"They did say it was an experience," Kate finally stated, and then quickly added, "We don't mean to be rude but we are anxious to see Blue."

"Oh dear, I am so sorry, of course you are," Vera answered sympathetically. "Let me call Nellie, I'm sure your little Blue will come too, they seemed quite taken with each other."

Sure enough, when Nellie's mistress called her name, she came in from another room, and there was Blue beside her, his tail straight up and looking very pleased with him self.

"Oh Blue, you had us so worried," Kate stooped down when he arrived at her feet and scooped him into her arms. He head butted her face and repeatedly meowed as if to make excuses for causing them so much distress. Without pulling from Kate's arms, he reached a paw toward Ell who of course wrapped his hand around it as if to say all was forgiven.

"He must be special," Vera spoke up, "Nellie has never brought home her beaus before."

Vera reached to rub her fingers down Blue's velvety back and he wrinkled his skin as if in distaste when she touched him. She raised her eyebrows at his reaction but said nothing.

"He's special to us," Ell returned. "Now, I believe we owe you a reward." Ell pulled out his billfold to extract the hundred dollar bill reserved for payment.

"Don't you dare, you put that away," Vera informed him, "I know how it feels to lose someone you care about. You keep your money, seeing he got back to his owners was payment enough."

"Well, thank you Vera," Ell said, "You are very kind and if we could return the favor sometime we will."

"Yes, well I'll remember that then," she replied as she opened the door for them to leave.

Ell and Kate silently walked to the van. She wrapped Blue in his blanket and settled him on her lap as they backed out of the drive. Kate couldn't get away from that woman fast enough. Her hand still itched from the contact.

CHAPTER 20

▼

Ell and Kate returned to the beach house with Blue. They barely had time to show mother waiting in the front hall that all was well before Keith and Todd were dragging them up to the gallery and the murder investigation. Kate whispered to Anne and Sam that she needed to speak with them later and they both nodded in consent.

"We laid them all out in order," Todd began, "and we even have some information out of the newspapers. He's from Texas; paper says his name is Eugene Blackford."

The gallery was sparsely decorated, two small stands with vases gelled to their tops like a museum does to avoid being knocked off, there were several framed watercolors and one large oil painting. The guys were afraid to tape the pictures on the wall for fear of pealing off the paint when it was removed, so the pictures were lined up along the wall on the floor.

Blue began to wiggle so Kate took him out on the landing, set him on the floor and draped his blanket across the railing. Blue ran back into the gallery and began walking in front of the pictures beside the men as though he was studying them. Kate pointed it out to her sisters and they started to giggle.

"Don't let Blue solve the crime before you can gentlemen," Sam giggled to their husbands and then the girls lost control and exploded into laughter.

Blue ignored them and studied each picture diligently trying to find a tell tale cause of the man's death. When he finally found what he was looking for, he backed up pulling it out from the rest with his front paws and then rolled across it, stretching out as if to say 'My work is done here'.

His fellow sleuths in the room all laughed thinking he was mighty picky which picture to lay on, until they themselves looked closer at the photo.

"Well, well, well," Keith stated as he also noticed what Blue had found.

"I don't see it," Kate was upset that she over looked something that a cat could pick up.

"There," Ell pointed out what now was obvious. "Good job Blue."

Blue didn't acknowledge the praise; instead he walked out onto the third floor landing. Now that his work was done, food and an afternoon nap had captured this thoughts and he headed for the bedroom.

"How could we have missed it yesterday morning?" Kate was still berating herself for not seeing it before now.

"Yesterday I think maybe we were more interested in our waffles," Anne volunteered.

"Oh, too true," Sam agreed.

"Well, we have the cause of death," Todd said, "Now we need to figure out who did it and why."

಄

"It's good to hear the kids back to normal." Mother was washing a load of clothes since they weren't going to be able to pack them right away.

Father was reading what he could of the butchered newspapers. It was a good thing he had read the beach murder articles on the way home from the grocery, or he wouldn't have got a chance. Three newspapers ran it on the front page and they picked up all three, the boys had cut the articles out as soon as they got back. "I wonder how long we'll have to stay here before ..." the house phone rang and interrupted father in mid-sentence, mother picked it up on the second ring.

"Hello?" Mother listened as the caller spoke and then she answered, "Yes it is. Is this Sheriff Poole?"

Father's eyes shot to the ceiling before whispering, "Does he have us bugged?"

Mother put her index finger to her lips to shush her husband then answered another question from the sheriff, "We didn't have plans for leaving today, so yes, we'll be here." She waited a few seconds then continued, "Three o'clock it is then, goodbye."

"Maybe we'll get to go home tomorrow," father knew he was too optimistic but tax payer's money was on the line.

"I know you don't like the situation we're being forced into, but I want you on your best behavior when he gets here. He's only doing his job." Mother gave him the look she normally used with the girls that said 'I'm not budging on this issue' until he finally agreed.

"Fine," father stated reluctantly, "but it'll cost you dinner, just the two of us, and I'm in the mood for steak."

"And, what about the kids, what are they going to do for dinner?" Mother grilled him, "We were just complaining we didn't get to see them as much as we like and here we are running off to have an evening alone."

"They know how to cook," father answered calmly, "besides, a relaxing evening alone with my best girl is what vacations are all about."

"No, our vacations are all about spending time with our daughters, whom we see very little of now that they've grown." Mother's hands had come to rest on her hips.

"There's no reason to get into a snit, we're going, so you better let the kids know and they can plan accordingly." Father had put his foot down, figuratively speaking.

Mother made her shoulders appear slumped as she headed upstairs to let the kids know. Marriage was a give and take process, you choose your battles, loosing this one was a win-win situation because she enjoyed special evenings with her husband. The two of them hadn't gone out for a date in a long time and the thought put a spring in her step.

Chapter 21

▼

"Good afternoon Sheriff Poole," Dexie insisted on being the one to answer the door when the sheriff arrived. "Won't you come in?"

"Thank you Mrs. Robertson," Sheriff Poole answered as Dexie escorted him to the family room where everyone was waiting.

"Call me Dexie, most everyone does," Dexie informed the sheriff.

"Of course, Dexie," he spoke her name hesitantly; making a mental note of *Dexie is not from Dixie* as a catch phrase to remember her name. He often did this due to the huge number of people he met everyday. He walked directly toward Jack with outstretched hand. "Jack, if I may call you that, good to see you."

Jack glanced toward his wife as she lowered her eyes and gave a slight nod of her head. "Of course, and let me introduce our children." Jack turned toward Anne who was sitting closest to him. "Anne is our middle daughter and this is her husband Keith, our youngest daughter Samantha and her husband Todd, and our oldest daughter Kate and her husband Ellsworth." Jack had stretched his arm out indicating each couple as he announced their lineage status.

"Nice to see all of you again," The sheriff nodded and then began. "Shall we all sit, this may take awhile. First of all, the station received a memory stick which had pictures of the coroner while he was excavating the body. None of you would have any idea how that envelope magically appeared on Sergeant Delano's desk do you?"

Keith spoke up first, "Sure sheriff, we dropped it off there. Everyone was busy so we just left it on one of the desks. We felt you should have them, were we wrong?"

Everyone's eyes were focused on the sheriff's reaction to Keith's very direct question. "Well of course we should have them. The question is why did you have them?"

"We took them while the coroner was excavating the body from the sand." Todd stated matter-of-factly. "We thought it would help in your investigation."

"You had no right to take those pictures and I must insist that if you have any copies of the pictures that you hand them over to me." The sheriff would expect nothing less than the extra copies of the pictures he was sure they had made and had in their possession.

"You are more than welcome to them sheriff," Keith hesitated before continuing, "You did find the cause of his death didn't you? We have a photo that unmistakably shows how he was killed. You have seen the photos, have you not?"

"I glanced at them briefly," the sheriff replied a little stiffly, "But the coroner has found the cause, yes."

"Let me run and get them," Todd volunteered and headed toward the stairs.

"You know sheriff," Ell spoke for the first time since the sheriff's arrival, "We, and by we I mean sisters and brother's-in-law, have come to the conclusion that Mr. Blackford was killed by a woman but we haven't figured out why."

The sheriff's eyebrows rose an inch on his forehead. "And why do you think it was a woman?" His own investigators only came to that decision an hour ago.

"I knew you would start without me," Todd said as he descended the last few steps, "you dirty dogs." He added good-naturedly.

Ell waited until Todd had handed the pictures to the sheriff with the one all knowing photo on top and then sat down. "As you can see in the photo here and here," Ell had gotten up and indicated on the photo just what he was talking about, "this edging, or what's left of it from crabs, shows where he was brought down to his knees by a taser, and his knees have a slight discoloration indicating the bruising from coming in contact with the boards on the end of the walk which you can see in another photo."

"But a taser only disables you; it doesn't kill anyone unless they have a heart condition." The sheriff had to admit that this group was smarter than the average person and very quick on the uptake.

"Our point exactly," Ell continued, "disabling him long enough to stab him in the base of his scull. We felt this was premeditated no matter how it appeared when it was first discovered."

"But you haven't explained why you think it was a woman." The sheriff figured he might as well hear everything before making his final decision as to whether they were nut cases or not.

"The guy was tall but not that big, one would think he was someone that stayed mainly behind a desk, so if it was a man that killed him he could have done it anywhere or moved him anywhere." Ell stopped to take a drink of his water before continuing. "No, a woman would have had to have him down to her height before she could kill him in that manner. Then she would need a way to cover or get rid of the body without having to move it. She probably was hoping the body would have stayed undiscovered for longer than it was." Ell finally stopped talking and sat down.

The sheriff was impressed with their accuracy and the amount of information they had uncovered. Much of it was parallel to the investigating team's report an hour earlier. "How did you come to this conclusion?"

Todd spoke before anyone else had a chance, "Amateur sleuth's sheriff, it's kind of a hobby of ours."

Silence fell over the room. Mother stood up and announced she was getting the coffee and cookies and quickly escaped to the kitchen.

Father volunteered to help and followed her out of the room.

Chapter 22

▼

After the sheriff left and they got mother and father shooed out the door for their 'date', the sisters called the sub shop in town, ordered a variety of sandwiches and sent their husbands out to get them. They stayed behind to make coffee, finish up some laundry and pack the things they wouldn't need over the next couple of days. They wanted to be able to leave as soon as the sheriff gave the okay. Their husbands came in the door with the submarine sandwiches just as they flipped the switch on the coffee maker.

"Ell, we've got skim milk, apple juice and water, which do you want with your sub?" Kate was standing in front of the open fridge as she rattled off items she knew Ell could drink.

"Water's fine." Then Ell added as an afterthought, "Check my pill box and see if I've already taken my pills for this evening. We've been so busy I can't remember if I took them or not."

"They're still in here," Kate held up the multi-compartment box, "I'll bring them over with our water. Hey, did mom already pack the napkins, I can't find them."

"Oh I saw those in the box," Sam offered, "it's still in the pantry on the floor, grab a handful, I know I'm going to get messy I had them put everything on my sandwich."

"Okay, I've got some information that we need to discuss and then decide what we can do with it." Kate took a bite of her sandwich and washed it down with a drink of water before she began. "The woman that called us about Blue was Vera Johnson."

"You mean that woman that hounded mom & dad at the casino?" Anne couldn't believe it. "How did she end up with Blue?"

"Apparently, Blue had followed her cat Nellie home and spent the night." Kate explained.

"That little Casanova," Sam commented.

"Well, she wanted to talk, mentioned meeting mom and dad at the casino, said how much she enjoyed talking with them and then," Kate paused to get a drink before continuing, "she tried to worm out of us how much money dad had won playing poker."

"You've got to be kidding," Anne said at the same time Sam stated, "How rude!"

"Oh she was trying to be nonchalant about it," Kate continued, "but that's what she was after. We finally had to just ask for her to get Blue."

"Mom said she was a talker and they couldn't get away from her," Anne replied. "She didn't say the woman was nosey too."

Kate nodded her head in agreement before going on, "When we mentioned we were staying at the 'Tiwardrai' beach house I noticed her tense up. So when we shook hands you wouldn't believe the evil vibes flowing off of her, it was phenomenal. I had another one of those 'red' visions, you know where everything is red, and a bunch of men's faces started floating into view, I counted nine of them before we broke contact. I think they're all dead because one of them looked like that Blackford guy, and when we offered to pay her the reward, she wouldn't hear of it and said 'maybe we could return the favor for her sometime'."

Having finished his sandwich Todd joined the conversation, "What do you think she meant by that?"

"I don't know," Kate answered, "but she gives me the creeps."

"I would think so," Sam agreed. "I think we need to tell the sheriff she's the killer."

"Yeah right Sam, like he's going to believe us," Kate exclaimed. "My visions are not proof no matter how accurate they seem to be."

"Okay then, how about we call the police from a pay phone and tell them to check her out?" Anne offered, "That woman has to be stopped before she kills again."

"Yeah, I like that idea," Ell joined the conversation. "Let's finish up here and head out to make the call before mom and dad get back. Come on Kate eat up!"

Kate gave him a frown but kept her opinions to herself as she took a second bite of her sandwich.

"I'll bring in the coffee if everyone is ready for it." Anne suggested.

"I'll help you, since Kate still has to finish," Sam followed Anne into the kitchen.

"Come on you guys, I'm eating as fast as I can," Kate replied with a mouth full of veggies and bun. She and Ell had ordered grilled veggie subs and it would have tasted better if she could have eaten it slower to enjoy the full flavor of the sandwich. Fresh veggies, a smear of tomato paste on a whole wheat bun, a sprinkle of oregano and mozzarella cheese all grilled to perfection was one of their favorite quick sandwiches. "I'll drink my coffee when we get back, that way I won't have to rush it too!"

"Hey, while we're out we probably should stop at the supermarket and pick up something for dinner tomorrow night. I can't see the sheriff letting us leave before then." Keith was thinking ahead as always, he knew his wife liked to plan her meals with plenty of time to change if needed.

"I thought you fell asleep on us Keith," Ell chided him. "You haven't said a word the whole time we were eating. Do you have an opinion on what we should do with this new information Kate has given us?"

"Only that Kate is right, they aren't going to believe us based on her visions, so that only leaves an anonymous call," Keith answered. "So let's get it done, we've got food to buy."

Chapter 23

"Where do you think it would be best to call from?" They were all piled into Ell and Kate's van just driving off the bridge that connected the island to the mainland. Ell needed a direction to go any further once they reached the stop light at the intersection.

"We can go into the new Food Lion over by Calabash or we can go into Shallotte to the super Wal-Mart." Ell kept his eye on the light, anticipating the change, "I think both places would be good cover for the phone call."

"Let's go to Shallotte," Anne said just as the light changed green. Ell swung the vehicle to the right and sped down Highway 178 toward Shallotte. "That way we can run into the Bath & Body Shop too, I'm almost out of lotion, and then I won't have to pick it up after we get back home."

"Oh, if we're going to be shopping I wouldn't mind going to Lowes and The Home Depot," Sam added.

"Lowes is clear out on I-17," Todd exclaimed.

"Do we have anything else planned for the evening?" Sam asked rather sarcastically.

"She's right Todd, we don't have anything in particular to do and I don't mind wandering around in a lumber yard. I rather like the smell of fresh cut lumber." Kate was remembering when she was small and would go with her mother to take father lunch into the lumber mill where he worked. That was many years ago, but the smell of wood always brought it back as if it were yesterday.

"Here we are," Ell unnecessarily stated as he pulled into the parking lot. "Does anyone know where the pay phone might be?"

"Probably down by the soda machines," Keith announced.

☙

"Yes, I would like to speak with someone working on the Eugene Blackford case." Kate turned to the group and gave the thumbs up. She was holding the receiver with a paper napkin she found in the glove box of the van, who knew how many germs were on a public phone. "Please listen carefully because I am only going to say this once. Recently I had the misfortune of meeting Vera Johnson; she lives on the island close to where the body was found. I got the distinct impression she was hiding something unpleasant. I think it would behoove your department to run a few checks on her." Kate hung up the phone without saying goodbye, wiped the front of the machine, and dropped the napkin in the trash bin as the group headed into the store. "Do you think they traced the call?"

"Probably," Anne answered, "so it was a good thing you didn't stay on the phone long."

"I think it takes two minutes to trace a call," Sam replied.

"Okay you three, stop worrying, we've got meals to buy for." Keith didn't want to spend all evening getting groceries if they were stopping at the other stores also.

"So, what do we want for lunch tomorrow?" Anne got out a notepad from her purse and began listing the items they would need as the group discussed different options.

"How about we fix a light pasta combination for lunch, and then something more substantial in the evening?" Sam was already thinking of which recipe she was going to fix for lunch. "We're going to need two pounds uncooked shrimp, a pound of fusilli pasta, they do have bulk pasta here don't they? Broccoli, red pepper, onion, fresh parsley, do we still have fresh grated parmesan back at the house? Oh, and we'll pick up a bottle of light Italian dressing instead of making it from scratch."

"Geez Sam, did you need any input from Anne and I?" Kate was a little put out since Sam just ran roughshod over them. "Does that mean we get to make the decision for the evening meal?"

"Sorry," Sam apologized, "I've been craving shrimp since the Red Lobster advertisement on television yesterday evening."

"Well, we are on the ocean where everything is fresh; one would expect to eat shrimp at least once while they were here." Anne spoke as she finished writing something on the list. "I've added a dessert to lunch; it's a chocolate and banana parfait. I figured we would need something sweet after that tangy pasta."

"It's not tangy," Sam interjected, "it's zesty!"

"Whatever," Anne returned. "Do we need any rolls with it?"

"I'll grab some sesame Italian rolls," Sam crossed her arms in a huff.

"If you ladies are going to argue over every little thing," Keith announced, "then we're going to the fishing and electronics departments. Come get us when you've got everything you need." The men took off in the opposite direction of the women.

"You two did a good job," Kate whispered as the men walked off. "I was beginning to think they were going to follow us clear through the food section."

"Good gracious, what a disaster that would have been," Sam stated. "Todd is always trying to add snacks we don't need, to the cart."

"Keith wants to compare everything." Anne added.

"That's better than, 'Do we really need that?' I get from Ell every time I pick something up," Kate offered.

"Men who normally don't do the cooking shouldn't be allowed to grocery shop with the wives who do," Sam announced. "Now, what were we going to fix for the evening meal?"

Chapter 24

After dumping ice into the cooler in the back of the van they left the Wal-Mart parking lot and headed to the plaza where Home Depot and the Bath & Body Shop were located. Anne ran in the store by herself to get the lotion while everyone else waited in the van before they drove across the plaza to Home Depot.

"Let's split up and meet back up front in forty-five minutes," Ell informed them as they climbed out of the van, "that will give us fifteen minutes to get to Lowes and still have nearly an hour there before they close."

The couples separated and headed toward the areas they were interested in. Kate and Ell were in the process of remodeling their bathroom and couldn't decide on floor coverings. Anne and Keith just finished their kitchen and were looking for an area rug as a point of focus to complement the room. Sam and Todd had recently decided to finish out a recreation room in their basement, so they were comparing prices. Of course, they all ended up in the garden center at the same time and left the store from there.

Heading out to Lowes, they somehow got on the subject of the Indianapolis 500. "I'm just saying they should get it back to what it was designed for, and that was pitting one car maker against another." Ell was very adamant about this. "They put such strict rules and regulations on the turbines that it took all the competitiveness out of the race. You might as well use wind-up toys as call that a competitive race."

"Oh good, we finally got here." Kate wanted to break the conversation up before it headed in the direction it always did with Ell, an argument over what they were competing against. "There's a good spot up by the Exit doors."

Ell whipped the van into the parking spot Kate had indicated and they all got out of the van and headed toward the entrance. "Shall we meet up by the registers before they close?" It was a rhetorical question, and Ell headed toward the raw lumber to cool off, Kate let him go ahead, giving him the space he so obviously needed.

※

Kate meandered slowly toward the open stock lumber section in the store. She would stop every so often looking at a sale item that grabbed her attention until finally, turning the corner to meet up with Ell.

"Look who I ran into," Ell said as Kate came around the corner at the end of the isle.

"Mom, Dad, we thought you were on a date," Kate exclaimed.

"Your father wanted to stop in and check prices on the building products," Mother replied. "He likes to keep up with costs. I'm glad we retired when we did; those prices are getting way out of hand. People are going to have a hard time with normal maintenance let alone with building a new home."

"They are a lot higher than a few years ago," Kate added. "Although, loan rates are at a new low so that helps a little bit."

"Not enough dear, not nearly enough," Mother answered.

"Hey, you guys have a strange idea for a date," Keith and Anne had came around the corner to find them talking.

"Well, you know, once it's in the blood it's hard to let go," Father informed them.

They all started to gravitate toward the flooring department when they bumped into Todd and Sam having a heated discussion on wall to wall carpeting or tile flooring for the basement.

"Dad! I should have known you two would end up at one of these stores while we were on vacation. How about telling Todd why tile flooring is best for the basement." Sam turned toward Todd fully expecting her father to agree with her side.

"Actually, you would probably be more satisfied with a laminate floor." Father's statement caught Sam off guard and she turned to face him as he continued. "You can put a layer of that new pre-formed insulation they are making from old tires down first before putting in the flooring and it'll also reduce the heat needed in that area."

"Hey, that sounds better yet," Todd replied.

"Yeah, thanks dad," Sam hugged her dad; she and Todd were finally making progress.

"I know a place where we can all get a great cup of coffee," Anne stated. "Is anybody interested?"

"Are we talking about Starbucks?" Kate could not believe her ears.

"Nope, Le French Press back at the beach house," Anne answered.

"I think I've already packed that," Mother began then hesitated, "no wait, I only set it on the dresser in our suite. Okay kids, let's go get that coffee."

Ell leaned toward Kate as they walked through the exit doors, "Did you have any of that hot chocolate left? I don't think I need caffeine this close to bed."

"Of course dear," Kate laid her hand on his arm, "I have hot apple cider mix too."

Ell's eyes lit up, he hadn't had any hot apple cider since the cook out last October. "I'll take the cider." He squeezed her hand still resting on his arm as they headed toward the vehicle.

Chapter 25

▼

"Did you get a trace?" Sheriff Poole was more than a little irritated. One of the few times he has ever stepped out of the office to get a bite to eat and something like this happens.

"No, the call was too short. All we got was the number and that it was a pay phone, which popped up on our caller ID." Officer Eric Boone hated to see the sheriff beat himself up for not being here, the sheriff worked hard and deserved a break once in a while. "The phone company said that it was the pay phone out at Wal-Mart, but by the time we got a dispatch out there, no one was around and no eye witnesses. The phone had been wiped clean of course."

"Well, I guess all we can do is follow-up on the lead and hope the caller wasn't a crack pot. Did you run any checks yet?" Sheriff Poole was massaging his forehead with his fingers, waiting for an answer.

"I was putting her name into the system as you arrived sir, it should be done by now," Officer Boone replied as he turned his chair back to face his computer screen. "*Hello!* Vera Johnson has been a busy little lady; have a look at this sir." He rolled his chair to the side so the Sheriff could get a better look at the computer screen.

Sheriff Poole exhaled loudly, "Who would have thought it. Print it off and start cross referencing Eric; I want results on my desk in two hours. I'm heading out to the local police station on the island to see what information I can get from that perspective and give them a heads up." Finally they were getting somewhere.

Chapter 26

Vera gave her most winning smile as she looked up at her newest conquest. His whole persona just oozed money and she couldn't wait to get her hands on it. She was sick and tired of scrimping and scraping just to keep up appearances. "Wasn't it a beautiful day Thaddeus?"

"It's rather windy now that the sun has gone down," Thaddeus complained; he was a frail man in his mid-seventies. He was dressed in khaki slacks, a cream polo with a chocolate sweater loosely tied around his neck to appear as though casually draped across his shoulders and tan deck shoes; a young look for a man his age.

"Why don't you let me help you with your sweater, I wouldn't want to be the cause of you getting a summer cold," Vera offered. They had driven down to the casino boat right after her early dinner. The sun had still been high when they got on the boat, but now as they walked across the parking lot toward her car the wind had picked up considerably and it caused chill bumps to rise on Thaddeus' arms. "We'll be back at my place in no time and if you like we could start a fire to keep us warm."

"That sounds lovely Vera," Thaddeus murmured then added hopefully, "and maybe a glass of brandy to warm our insides as well?"

"You read my mind Thaddeus; we are so much alike." Vera smiled sweetly as she patted Thaddeus' hand lying on his leg. Vera put the car in gear and pulled out of the parking lot with dollar signs spinning in her head. "How long do you have for vacation Thaddeus?"

"I'm planning on moving here," Thaddeus stated, "I'm checking out the neighborhoods. I thought Cherry Grove Island would be a good place to land, but there's too many thirty-five to forty year olds. I spent three days there, in the middle of the week mind you, and there was nothing but noisy parties every night. That's not the kind of environment I want to live in."

Vera's eyebrows shot straight up, Cherry Grove property sold in the millions, how much was he worth if that property was an option? Vera slowly let out the breath she had unknowingly been holding, "They do have a motorcycle week there every year and it seems most of the people I've seen there are the younger executive types, but I'm sure you'll find something that will take your fancy." Vera promised herself it would be her, which meant she needed to play hardball a lot quicker than she had planned.

"I suppose you are right," Thaddeus replied. "Say, how about we run up the coast tomorrow and check out Bald Head Island, I've heard some nice things about it."

"That would be a two day trip to do the island justice Thaddeus," Vera exclaimed, "You would need to check in with your family to let them know, I don't think your cell phone will work out there." Vera was hoping against hope he had no family ties and found herself holding her breath until he answered.

"That's not a problem Vera; I don't need to let anyone know where I am," Thaddeus answered matter-of-factly.

Vera nearly fainted with relief, he was perfect: lots of money and no one to fight over the estate when he died. "No one should be alone, Thaddeus. I myself despise being alone."

"You get used to it," Thaddeus began. "My wife and I were high school sweethearts. We were unable to have children but we were satisfied with just having each other. When they found cancer in her lymph nodes, she was one month short of fifty-six; she died before she turned fifty-seven. I've been alone ever since." Thaddeus sighed, "Life is hard and we don't always get what we want, but if you enjoy what you have when you have it, somehow it keeps you going when you don't."

Vera was silent. Thaddeus had hit a raw nerve; one she thought had long healed over. Her first husband had loved her passionately but all she could think of while he was alive was money, when he died she felt cheated. Would her life have turned out differently if she had enjoyed the time they had together, but then again, could she have gone on alone?

Chapter 27

▼

Sheriff Poole arrived at the Islands' only Police station to find Officer Jeremy Cross busy on the computer at the only work desk up front. His name plate was slightly skewed and the sheriff straightened it before he began talking.

"When will your partner be checking back in?" Sheriff Poole knew two officers were always on duty at this post.

"If nothing holds him up, he should be back momentarily. Got something big sheriff?" Officer Cross was a new transfer from Illinois, and very eager to move up in the ranks.

"I'd prefer to talk to both of you at the same time so I don't have to repeat myself." Sheriff Poole answered.

"Well, there's fresh coffee in the back if you'd like." Officer Cross turned back to finish the last few sentences on his report. He printed a copy to sign and drop off at headquarters on his way home, and then saved and sent the one on the computer to the appropriate document folder on the hard drive. He was just putting the signed copy into an interoffice envelope as the sheriff returned to the front.

"Pretty fancy coffee machine you got back there," Sheriff announced before continuing, "How'd you justify that in the budget?"

"Lieutenant Braddock brought that in; he bought a new one for home. It does make a mean cup of coffee; of course it helps if you grind fresh beans first." The young officer missed the Sheriff's snort of disgust at the comment when his attention was drawn to the squad car pulling in the parking lot, "Right on schedule," he announced as an officer in his late thirties got out of the car, "the Island must be back to normal now that the holidays are over."

"I wish it was," Sheriff Poole murmured to himself.

CR

Lieutenant James Braddock was in shock. Oh, the Island has an occasional accidental death and until this last death no murders, but for one of the original builders to be considered a murderer was more than he wanted to accept. The Lieutenant grew up in North Carolina and visited all of the Islands numerous times, but this one was his favorite. Before putting in a request for this job, he worked with the State Troopers on highway patrol plus transferred inmates back in State from out-of-state jurisdictions.

"I can't believe it, she and her husband were among the first people to build on the Island. Vera was one of the first women to win a gold medal in the Olympics when she was younger. She owns three properties now you know," he began to reminisce, "Vera and her husband put up several birdhouses when I was quite young and I thought it strange since the only birds I ever saw were too big to fit in any houses they had. Eventually, she changed the single birdhouses into bird hotels. She has one on each property she owns, kind of like a trademark. Someone comes once a year to clean them out, repair any damage and paint them if needed to match the beach house they go with." Lieutenant Braddock gave himself a mental shake, "Just goes to show you never really know some people, who would have thought it. She's still a good looking woman; I expect that's how she attracts all those men. Man I hate for something like this to happen here."

"We all do Lieutenant, we all do," Sheriff Poole agreed and sympathized.

"I'd like to be with you when you question her, I want to be involved with anything that goes down on the island, and it's still my beat." Lieutenant Braddock announced boldly.

It was a statement not a request and the sheriff knew it, but he accepted it. "That's understandable and I have no problem with you accompanying me." He would have felt the same if the tables were turned, plus it's always good public relations to work well with the individual corporate Police stations. "I'll give you a call when we get everything in place." The Sheriff shook hands with the Lieutenant, "It's good to have you aboard."

Chapter 28

▼

Sunday morning arrived bright and sunny. Blue had been head butting his human companions for a good ten minutes before finally meowing loudly in Kate's ear. Not quite awake, Kate dragged herself over to the bedroom door and let Blue out of the room to wreck havoc elsewhere in the beach house. The doors were secure so Kate felt he couldn't get into trouble in the time it would take her to shower.

Blue sped to the third floor and jumped up on the window ledge to scan the beach for Nellie. It had only been one day but he already missed her. She was nowhere in sight.

He leapt from the window and ran down the stairs two at a time, sounding more like several cats than just one, arriving at the back door only to find it closed. Jumping onto a small table situated in front of one of the many windows facing the beach he pushed his head through the draperies to check the deck. The object of his desire was lying on the bench sleeping.

Blue yelled a greeting that would have deafened anyone standing next to him. Nellie opened her eyes and allowed them to focus before answering him back. She stood up and stretched, arching her back high like a Halloween cat. Blue stretched too.

Nellie walked down the bench and sat in front of the window Blue was behind, unsure what to do next. Blue stood and put his front paws on the glass and meowed. Nellie answered with a lighter mew. Blue jumped back down on the floor and ran to Mother and Father's chambers so fast he turned sideways skidding on the tile floor and crashed against their door.

Mother was ready to open the door when he landed with a thud. "Blue where are you headed in such a hurry?" She looked at him waiting for a reply.

Blues' answer was a sharp meow as he turned and ran back across the room, stopping half way to look back and see if she was following. Noticing she was still standing in the same place he gave her another sharp meow and waited for her to move.

"Oh I see, you want me to follow you," Mother stated before taking a step. "I must say, Kate never told us you were so demanding. What is it you need Blue? Peanut butter? A bowl of milk? Maybe some canned tuna."

But Blue walked past the kitchen and headed back to the window he had just vacated. He poked his head out the draperies again to reassure himself Nellie was still waiting. She was and he gave her a reassuring mew to let her know he was getting someone to help.

Mother opened the draperies to allow the light to fill the rooms and noticed Nellie sitting on the deck bench. "Blue, it appears you have a visitor. Shall I let her in?" To which mother received a loud meow. Opening the inside door, Blue was pawing at the glass before mother knew it. She bent down and scooped him into her arms before opening the door and allowing Nellie in to visit. Setting Blue back onto the floor next to Nellie she secured the door before heading in to start breakfast for her family. Today, she was fixing the Blue Flower Chive Omelet. They had picked up the ingredients last night and she couldn't wait to get started.

Blue and Nellie headed upstairs to get a bite to eat before stretching out in the sun in the Gallery. The film on the gallery windows designed to keep the harmful rays from doing any damage to the paintings worked out perfect for Blue. It allowed him to sun as long as he wanted without getting his skin burned.

Kate was coming down the stairs as Blue and Nellie were going up. "Good morning Blue, good morning Nellie," Kate stated as she passed them on the steps. The two cats mewed but kept moving forward as if they had been together for a lifetime; both their bodies in sync with the others'. Kate was glad she had left the door slightly opened when she left; Ell was still asleep and he probably wouldn't have heard Blue yelling to get in. Kate knew Ell's body was trying to catch up on the sleep he had missed the night before when he watched over her while Blue was gone. 'Lord refresh Ell's body as he sleeps,' Kate prayed silently as she stepped off the bottom stair and headed toward the smell of fresh hot coffee. She was joined by her father as his nose picked up on the fresh brew.

"Good morning," Father greeted her before adding, "That coffee smells awfully good, don't you think?"

"I'll say," Kate replied. "Did you get a good nights rest after being up so late?"

"You bet," Father answered, "We got in the Jacuzzi before going to bed, and it was quite relaxing."

"I've heard they can do wonders for tired muscles," Kate stated as they walked into the kitchen.

"What does wonders on tired muscles?" Mother had caught Kate's remark.

"The Jacuzzi dear," Father informed her as he winked.

The blood in Mother's cheeks heightened slightly before she announced, "I'm doing breakfast this morning, so just get a cup of coffee and I'll call you when it's ready."

"Do you need any help?" Kate inquired.

"No, go enjoy your coffee on the deck, I've got everything under control," Mother said.

"Okay, but Sam, Anne and I have got lunch and dinner planned out so you won't need to worry about that," Kate announced. "We figured the sheriff wouldn't be letting us go until Monday so we picked up a few things."

"Are you sure you don't want any help for the evening meal?" Mother turned toward Kate waiting for her answer.

"We'll see," Kate told her. "You might want to take that time to finish packing."

"You sound pretty sure of yourself." Mother replied. Kate just smiled as she walked out.

Chapter 29

Gospel singing accompanied by a tambourine and a small keyboard drifted softly on the breeze. The Sunday morning Beach Church was on this end of the island today. Except for heavy rain they held Gospel services every Sunday morning on the beach, welcoming anyone who wished to attend. The group was far enough away, you needed binoculars to see them, but the song drifted along the breeze for all to hear. Kate sang along to a song she hadn't sung since Grandmother Bolton's death. 'I'll fly away' had been one of grandma's favorites, she felt the author had said it all in three short verses written to uplift one's soul and remind them of their rewards.

"Grandma sang this song all the time; it reminds me a lot of when I was growing up." Kate was reminiscing more than talking to her father. She had closed her eyes and was thinking back of more simple carefree days.

"Breakfast will be ready in twenty minutes, let the others know." Mother had slipped out the door without either of them knowing it and had startled both of them.

"I'll get them in gear," Kate said once her vision had refocused. "Dad, you just enjoy the morning, we'll all be down in a few minutes."

"No problem," Father answered then added, "Life moves too fast, I need to catch up."

Kate turned to look at her father and laid her hand on the arm of his chair, "Is something wrong dad?"

"No honey," Father reached over and patted Kate's hand, "I was just stating a fact and regretting that life demands more from you now than it used to. Life used to be so much simpler. Now, go get your sisters."

Kate wondered if he was a mind reader. She gave herself a mental shake to clear such thoughts before kissing her father on top of the head and going into the house.

CR

The coffee had evidently woken everyone and had them preparing for the day. Even Ell was just drying off from his shower when she entered the room. She refilled the food and water bowls and cleaned the litter box before washing her hands.

"I noticed Blue has his girlfriend over this morning. She's quite the looker isn't she?" Ell was standing in front of the mirror with shave foam on his face, waiting on Kate to finish so he could continue.

"She is very pretty, and Blue seems to be smitten with her. I don't know how he will take it when we leave." Kate dried her hands on the towel and moved out of his way.

"I'm sure he'll manage," Ell said.

Kate walked over and began pulling the sheets off the bed. "I'm taking these sheets and pillow cases down to get them in the washer before Sam and Anne have the same idea. Come on down when you're done but leave the door open for Blue and Nellie." Kate was stuffing the sheets in the washing machine when she noticed Sam and Anne lugging their things down the steps to wash.

"Great minds, huh sis?" Sam dropped her load on top of the washing machine and Anne put hers on top the dryer. "Breakfast smells wonderful."

"It sure does. I'm pouring, so who wants coffee?" Anne had made a beeline toward the kitchen with her sisters close behind.

"Everything is ready." Mother passed the girls on her way to the table with napkins and the butter, "Help me get the table set and we can start eating."

Chapter 30

Vera and Thaddeus had talked until nearly midnight before Thaddeus headed back to his hotel alone, but they were planning on driving up the coast after lunch to spend a few days. Thaddeus had dominated most of the evening talking of his late wife; he was not looking for a wife but a companion to spend time with. Vera was okay with that and planned her strategy to be just that person for him. Besides, she was bound to out live him and maybe by then she could get palimony out of his estate if not everything.

Thaddeus' talk last night had Vera second thinking her method for achieving a comfortable living without working. She had deeply cared for several of her husbands and had grown fond of the rest, but the money never lasted long enough. The ones she disposed of in the septic tank she never even received insurance claims for and now since every one on the island has had to change to the new sewer system she had to get more creative with her deaths for husbands who got on her nerves before a decent time had lapsed. Even that nosy investigator had her pegged when his casino whales began disappearing, he really had to go. He would have spoiled everything.

Although Vera had orchestrated many accidents to occur while she and her husbands were vacationing and she had changed insurance companies with every husband; too many reported accidents would throw up a red flag. She was surprised the police hadn't caught on yet with all the computers and new technology used to keep tabs on people. Also, hind site told her she probably should have moved around periodically in neighboring States instead of living in one place, but she just couldn't let this house go. It was her first home and she had grown too attached to it. *'Hopefully that decision would not come back to haunt her,'* Vera thought.

So Vera decided if she played her cards right, Thaddeus would be the last. He obviously had enough money to last her a life time and maybe she wouldn't have to kill him to get what she deserved in life.

Chapter 31

▼

It was midnight. The sheriff had just disappeared down the street leaving his deputy in an unmarked car to watch the suspect's house. An older gentleman came out of the house and drove away. The deputy made a note of his departure on the laptop and sent the information to headquarters. The sheriff had already run the plate numbers of both vehicles parked at the house.

The gentleman leaving was Thaddeus Julian Brisbane, more than likely the suspect's next intended victim. He was a self made multi-billionaire, getting into the steel industry early and getting out just before the decline of its need. He had a knack for purchasing real estate before it blossomed into high dollars. Now retired, he lives off the interest his billions generate. They say he collected gold without a paper trail when he was younger. This was due to the fact that in 1933 President Roosevelt recalled all gold bullion to be turned in to the government or risk prosecution. That order could be issued again, even now and with gold currently at nearly one thousand dollars an ounce, one brick alone could be worth millions. The sad truth is, no one knows if the story is true or not. But if it is, to be his relative would set you up for life when he died, even dividing it up among multiple relatives.

The house had gone dark and the young deputy sighed before he settled back for a long watch. As the night released its hold to morning and blood red fingers stretched across the sky, a cat appeared on the hood of his car. It stared at him through the windshield. It peered down into the seat and then looked in the back before returning its stare to the officer. The cat emitted a piercing scream before jumping down and disappearing up the street. It had unnerved him to the point that by daylight, he had eaten everything he had packed, finished off his thermos of coffee, plus a can of energy drink he brought just in case he felt sleepy and he was still on edge. He liked cats, he grew up with them and has one now since moving into an apartment on his own, but he had never had an experience with one like this. The young officer was relieved when his replacement arrived early.

Nellie had been watching the man in the car for hours. She had seen the car parked there last night when the gentleman visiting her caregiver had left. Nellie had got situated on the window ledge after the lights were turned out to keep an eye on him. She watched him all through the night; it made her hairs stand out just to know he was watching them, but worst of all it made her feel something bad was going to happen.

By the time most of the night creatures were finishing up their rituals and heading back to their burros or nests, Nellie couldn't sit still any longer. She ran out through the flap on her door and across the sand dunes to the house just past where the vehicle was parked. She crept up behind the car and sniffed the bumper and tires to get an idea who it was. She checked the drivers' door and picked up the scent of someone with a cat of his own, but it didn't make her feel any less tense. Walking to the front of the vehicle she jumped to the hood and stared at the man inside. He seemed startled to say the least. Good, because she wanted to be the one in control for the moment. Glancing across the front seat, then the back, she returned her intense stare to the man. Taking in a deep breath of air first, she wailed out an ear splitting scream to put this intruder in his place.

Fully satisfied she had unnerved him to no end and he now knew where he stood in her neighborhood, Nellie jumped to the ground and ran up the street. Her senses were telling her something was truly wrong and the only place she felt she could quell them at this moment was with Blue.

Going to bed shortly after Theodore left, Vera was hard pressed to fall asleep. Her mind was racing with all the plans for getting her newest conquest wrapped around her little finger. If Theodore only wanted a companion then that would be her next goal. This was a new direction for Vera but she was willing to try anything once. Besides, if it didn't work out she could file for palimony, she figured he was rich enough he would never miss a few million.

Vera knew she had finally come to the crossroads in her life between rich and just getting by. She slipped into a deep restful sleep just before three-thirty, satisfied life was about to change in her favor and she would get everything she deserved.

Chapter 32

It was nearly noon by the time Sheriff Poole had chased down Judge Stevens to sign the warrant to search Vera Johnson's beach house. He was sure they would find the one thing she would have kept without thinking and it would nail her for the death of Eugene Blackford. The Sheriff had been in touch with the home office of the casino in Little River and knew Blackford had his suspicions of a Vera Mae Johnson residing on this island and had made note to contact her.

Sheriff Poole was getting a prickly feeling about this woman and once they charge her for this murder, they'll start checking on all those accidents with past husbands. Plus dig a little deeper and see if there is a connection to the missing men on the Blackford list.

The Sheriff stopped at the police station on the island to let Lieutenant Braddock know he was on his way to the suspect's house. Following the Sheriff, Braddock drove his own car down the main street to Vera's house. The Sheriff motioned for the Deputy still on duty watching the Johnson house to follow them to the door. The knot in the pit of Braddock's stomach that had first arrived with the news from the Sheriff, twisted tighter when they knocked on Vera's door; he really liked her, he hated that it had come to this.

"Hello Lieutenant, Sheriff, what seems to be the trouble?" The smile on Vera's face when she opened her door was soon replaced with what appeared to be shock when the Sheriff told her they had a warrant.

"We have a warrant to search your property in connection with the death of Eugene Blackford, Ms. Johnson," the Sheriff told her as he handed her the legal form justifying and allowing them to take any and all pertinent items for said case. "We will need for you to step outside with this officer please." The Sheriff held the door open for a bewildered Vera to walk through and then shut it before telling the Lieutenant what they were looking for specifically, although anything they felt that might appear to be connected to the case was to be bagged also.

Within fifteen minutes he had what he came for and returned to inform Vera she would need to come down to the station to answer some questions.

"I assure you Sheriff, I've done nothing wrong." Vera stated firmly, as though she were talking through clenched teeth. Her eyes hardened when she saw what he was holding in the zipped bag; it was her taser, "I only have that for self defense."

"If that is so, then it will all come out in the wash won't it Ms. Johnson?" Sheriff Poole was not giving her the chance to make a run. He planned to hold her on suspicion of murder while the forensics team combed the house from top to bottom.

"How long will it take, I've got a busy schedule today?" Vera hadn't moved an inch.

"I think your schedule has changed Ms Johnson, if you'll allow me?" Sheriff Poole stated as he took hold of her upper arm to guide her to the squad car.

"Unhand me sir, I can walk perfectly fine on my own," Vera spat venomously and jerked her arm from him, before stalking off toward the police car and climbing into the back seat.

Sheriff Poole informed Lieutenant Braddock he would keep him in the loop. Turning to the Deputy he made arrangements for him to stay on watch until the forensic team could arrive. Then got in behind the steering wheel of the squad car and drove off to the county jail.

꩜

The knot in Braddock's stomach began to ease, as he climbed into his car and drove back to the station. When life threw a curve ball like this it wasn't good trying to quit smoking *and* loose a few pounds.

Cross was finishing up on the morning report as Braddock strode toward his desk, "What happened? Are you any closer to the killer?"

Braddock grabbed the phone, pushed the speed dial number for a favorite restaurant and ordered a large pizza with everything and a two liter of soda to be delivered. A day like today would test even the toughest soul. Cross's eagerness was too much for Braddock at the moment so he turned to Cross's expected gaze and stated, "I hope you're in the mood for pizza." Then without giving him an opportunity to answer he headed to the back room for a strong cup of coffee; hoping the rest of the day would get a little bit easier.

Officer Cross shook his head, they had eaten lunch just over an hour ago, but he wasn't one to complain if the Lieutenant was paying for a pizza with the works. After all, whatever was left he would get to take home since Braddock's wife would hit the roof if she knew he had pizza. He was nearly at his weight goal. Jeremy pushed the save button and sent the report off to headquarters. He hated being stuck at the desk, maybe the time was right to ask for some of that field cruise time the Lieutenant had been promising.

Chapter 33

Lunch was long gone, the kitchen was clean and everyone was on the beach except the cats. Blue was trying to console Nellie, she had finally broke down and told him of her fear about being alone. A feeling that something dreadful was going to happen and that she would be forgotten and left on her own.

Blue nudged her face and they rubbed noses, and told her that he wouldn't let that happen. He would stow her away in the van if he had too. Nellie calmed down enough to fall asleep and Blue snuggled up next to her. Stretching his front leg across her shoulders, he laid his chin on top of her head and drifted off to those exciting places cats go when they sleep leaving them oblivious to all that surrounded them.

☙

The men were just coming out of the water when the women met them on the beach. The women had been collecting some of the olive shells that show up along the edge of the water. They had ended up with quite a few and only had to throw two back into the water because they still had residing occupants.

Anne had found one three inches long and as big around as your thumb. She had been worried she would go home without finding one that size. Sam had found one earlier in the week and had teased her dreadfully with it, as only sisters can.

Kate was only collecting the tiny ones this year to make a miniature shell jar for her curio cabinet so Sam couldn't tease her, but then there's always next year to get your sister. Life always presented you with wonderfully new opportunities.

"You guys look refreshed," Mother commented, "is the water cold?"

"Only at first," Father answered. He had salt water running off the hem of his swimsuit and down through the hairs on his legs to pool around his feet. "You girls should get in the water, it really is invigorating." Father had directed his statement toward his daughters only, his wife nearly drowned when she was younger and refuses to get into water deeper than her knees. But she had insisted her daughters learn at an early age.

"Maybe later dad," Anne was the weaker of the sisters at swimming and usually only swam in man made pools where there was no surf to push you about. "I was in the water earlier this week besides all the wading we did to find those welks we have up on the deck."

"How about you two," Father asked Kate and Sam.

Sam looked toward Kate, "The usual bet?" Sam began peeling off her cover-up as soon as she placed her few shells in Mothers hand.

Kate dropped her shells in the sand and pulled her cover-up over her head and tossed it on top of the shells. "I may be seven years your senior but I'm not old yet," Kate spouted at her sister as she ran for the water.

"That's not fair; I had more shells than you!" Sam complained good-naturedly as she ran two steps behind Kate.

"No excuses," Kate yelled triumphantly as her foot stepped in the water seconds before Sam. "You asked for this bet and you lost, and after a week on the beach my feet need a good massage before we leave." Since the sisters had gotten older, they had decided that a service chosen by the winner was a great benefit to not only the winner but it humbled the looser as well. So Kate chose the foot massage; but not just a regular massage, it was a thirty dollar reflexology session that lasted half an hour. Kate laid out her demands, "Thanks sis; I'll take that massage just before bed tonight please."

Sam splashed water toward her sister, "Stop gloating, next time I'll win!"

"Maybe, and then again, maybe not!" Kate teased Sam before she took off swimming into the waves.

Sam turned to ask Todd if he was heading back up to the house and was startled by him standing so close. "How did you sneak up on me?"

"You were arguing with your sister," Todd replied.

"We were not arguing," Sam snapped, "It's a sisters' thing, you wouldn't understand."

"And I don't plan on trying," Todd stated. "Let's swim, it may be our last time this year." They headed out toward Kate, when they got to her Todd continued. "I'm hoping the Sheriff gets things wrapped up before too long and we can head home. I saw the police walking around down at that Johnson woman's house a while ago. They must have her in custody."

"Hey, there comes the Sheriff now," Sam nodded her head toward a lone figure walking in the sand headed to their parents. "Swimming is over, let's go find out what he wants."

The swimmers reached shore just as the Sheriff met with the others waiting on the beach. "We have Ms Johnson in custody at the county jail. The only people she has asked to talk to is you two." The sheriff nodded his head toward Kate and Ell.

"Why would she want to talk to us, we barely know her," Ell questioned.

"She wouldn't say," Sheriff Poole replied, "She just kept asking to see you, got very adamant about it too."

"Well dear, we better get changed and head over to the jail to find out," Ell stated. "We'll drive over ourselves sheriff; you don't have to wait around for us." Then he added, "Give us about forty-five minutes; we'll need to get this salt water washed off."

Kate picked up her things before she and Ell walked back to the house. They rinsed the sand off their feet with the outside sprayer that hung beside the deck shower, grabbed towels hanging on the railing and disappeared inside the house.

"What's going on Sheriff," Father began, "surely you know something."

"Not a whole lot, but maybe it would be better if all of you came down to the office," the Sheriff stated.

"Does this mean we'll be able to leave for home anytime soon?" Father was ready to hit the road.

"Let's hope so; see you all in an hour." The Sheriff turned and walked back toward the house. He still needed to stop in at the Johnson house and get an update on the search, and then give Lieutenant Braddock his update on all that's happened since the arrest.

CHAPTER 34

Everyone squeezed into Ell and Kate's van, with the exception of Blue, whom they left behind sleeping with Nellie in the gallery. Kate didn't have the heart to separate them and put Nellie out. She hoped they behaved themselves and didn't have any accidents.

Ell and Kate couldn't figure out why Ms. Johnson had requested to see them, they barely knew her and what they did know of her wasn't something you boasted about to your friends. How anyone could not have a conscience eating away at them after the death of a loved one was beyond their realm of thinking. But to be the cause of someone's death and consider it as though you were getting rid of an insect would be unconscionable.

The drive to the county jail took longer than expected. This was an area most vacationers don't get to see and it was amazing how this county had set up the whole county government in one huge circle. To the unsuspecting vacationing family driving down the Old Coastal Highway, the circle was hidden from view behind giant pine trees and shrubbery; all planned that way for sure.

Pulling into the parking lot, everyone climbed out of the vehicle and headed toward the jail. This time of year the flowerbeds and shrubbery were in full bloom and quite beautiful to the eye. They obviously had it landscaped at some expense and keep a gardener on the staff. That cost to tax payers is enough to send you screaming in the opposite direction when looking to relocate for retirement. Although North Carolina is one of the oldest states in America, these buildings are fairly new. In particular the County Courthouse which was completed in two thousand two and is now too small for the population growth even with its six courtrooms.

Stepping through the door they were met by the receptionist. "May I help you?"

"We were asked by the Sheriff to come down and talk with someone you have in one of your holding cells. She is evidently asking to speak with us." Ell had expected the Sheriff to be up front anticipating the time of their arrival.

"Oh yes, he did say he was expecting you, let me give him a buzz." The receptionist lifted the phone receiver and pushed a speed dial button. "Those people you were expecting have arrived." She raised her eyes to glance at someone coming in the door, before continuing her conversation on the phone. "Yes sir, no I'll take care of it." The woman replaced the phone to its cradle, asked the gentleman who had just entered the door to take a seat and she would be right with him, before turning to the small group in front of her desk. "If you will go to that door over there I will buzz you in and Sheriff Poole will join you."

The small group did as they were asked and walked through the door to meet the Sheriff. "Since we were going to talk to all of you we figured putting you in an interrogation room would be best. Ell, Kate follow me, we have Ms. Johnson in a room with a phone and glass to separate you." Sheriff Poole walked down a hall and opened a door allowing Ell and Kate to enter the room before he shut it behind them.

Kate moved the chair facing the glass and Vera Johnson so she and Ell could hold the phone between them. Ell began the conversation, "We understand you wanted to see us Ms. Johnson."

"Yes young man. It seems I may be gone for quite a while and I was wondering if I could call in that favor you mentioned yesterday," Vera cleared her throat before continuing. "I'm sure you never thought you would be called on to honor that favor, but I am in a bit of a bind, and you appear to me to be good loving people."

When Kate and Ell remained quiet Vera continued. "I would like for you to take my Nellie to live with you. She got along with your Blue so well that I feel she would settle down much easier than if the authorities took her to the Humane Society. I don't think I could stand it if she was put in that place, she would be so unhappy."

Kate answered before Ell had a chance to refuse, "Of course we'll take Nellie, we couldn't allow her to be dumped without a care, not knowing if she would be put in a loving home or not." Ell turned and looked at Kate as she talked, not sure if he wanted another cat.

Vera seized on Kate's acceptance and ran with it. "You'll need to get her food and dishes from the house, her bed and travel case, what ever toys you think she might want and her litter hut, I had it made especially for her, it holds the litter pan and extra litter, make sure you take the whole thing, you'll find it is most handy at hiding everything out of sight from visitors." Vera mumbled on, "I'm not sure what will happen to the houses, I had them all double mortgaged; I suppose they will revert back to the mortgage companies."

"I'm sure we'll have to clear it with the sheriff before taking anything out of the house," Ell finally spoke up, resigning himself to the new addition to the family.

"I'll talk to him also and let him know I asked you to do this." Vera had already decided that she was not going to fight the law if she could get this couple to take Nellie. All her life she had known the consequences going into each adventure and she was getting too old to keep up with this life style much longer. It was a matter of time really. "Well then, that should be it. Nellie likes lots of sun to sleep in, please give her hugs for me, and tell her I'm sorry." At that Vera stood and hung up the phone.

She had turned her back to Kate and Ell but had not walked over to the door to be taken back to her cell. Kate knew Vera was trying to get hold of her emotions before moving on and felt just a small pang of sympathy for her, but it soon disappeared when she remembered all those men Vera cold-heartedly removed from this life.

Ell and Kate stepped out of the cubicle they had been in while talking to Vera and an officer returned them to the room with the rest of their family. The sheriff had just finished with the others when Kate and Ell entered the room.

"What did she want?" Sam asked the question before anyone else could.

"She wants us to take Nellie home with us," Kate was still a little stunned, as was Ell.

☙

Ell dropped off everyone except Kate at the beach house. Her sisters were going to get things started for the evening meal, and mother and father were going to finish their walk on the beach while they returned to Ms. Johnson's house to get Nellie's things. The sheriff was there waiting on them when they pulled up in the van.

"I'm not sure how large this litter hut is Sheriff, but if it's anything like the ones they show on the television that they convert from cabinets and dressers it will take three people to move it even if it's empty," Ell mentioned. "Have you got someone to spare that can help us move it?"

"I let the Island police know what was happening, Lieutenant Braddock will be here in a few minutes to help." The Sheriff obviously did not plan on helping to lift the cabinet.

Entering the house, Kate looked to the sheriff for instructions of what directions to go in to get to the cat's room. "Take the stairs to the second floor and turn right, it's the only room on that end of the upper level." The sheriff walked over to one of his men working in the house gathering evidence and stood talking to him as Kate and Ell headed upstairs.

The room was nothing Kate or Ell had ever seen even on television specials. It was a shame Nellie would be loosing such a wonderful place. Kate picked up the bed and blankets to shake out while Ell headed toward the food bowls and searched for the shut off on Nellie's water fountain. They took all the items out to the van with the exception of the litter hut. They emptied out the hut; it had as Vera mentioned the litter pan, extra litter and two scoopers in an upper drawer. They showed the sheriff the items that were in the cabinet. The litter in the lined box appeared as though Nellie hadn't used it in quite a while, which was probably true since she had a pet door to go outside. This litter box would only be used on rainy days that she would be cooped up inside the house. The sheriff looked at the box and dismissed it, however he did open the extra litter container and sifted through it to make sure nothing was hidden inside it before they took it on outside.

Lieutenant Braddock showed up as Ell and Kate were ready to bring down the hut. Kate carried the drawer that ran across the full length at the top. The sheriff hurriedly looked over the cabinet; informed them off handedly that they were free to head back home in the morning, and then allowed them to take the cabinet on out and put it in the van.

Kate made Ell rest in the van while she went back in and got the canned food Vera had stored in the kitchen downstairs, the dry had been stored up in Nellie's room. Kate thanked the sheriff and returned to the van, where she thanked the Lieutenant and wished him luck on the investigation before driving back to their own beach house.

The van would have to be rearranged to accommodate this pie safe size cabinet for the ride home. She would let her husband and her brothers-in-law figure it all out; surely they wouldn't have to rent a trailer to get everything home.

Kate dismissed the van packing from her mind as she headed in to the kitchen to wash up and help her sisters get started on the evening meal. She was so ready for a good meal and that foot massage tonight.

Chapter 35

▼

"The grill is heating up, have they found anything at the Johnson place yet?" Of course it was Sam bombarding Kate, and wanting details on the forensic investigation. Anne stood with her back against the countertop drinking a glass of sun tea, unusually quiet.

"I have no idea," Kate replied. "The sheriff didn't allow anyone to talk to us while we were there, and he didn't do much of it either. He examined everything we took out, including the tub of extra litter, however he dismissed the used litter box. I have no idea what he was looking for, a weapon of some kind I suppose, but he found nothing."

"You said Ms. Johnson insisted you take the litter hut with you, what does it look like?" Anne finally spoke up, hoping for a description of this odd sounding piece of furniture.

"Do you remember that old pie safe mother got out of our Great Aunt Daisy's house when dad remodeled it?" Kate had raised her eyebrows at the end of her question.

"Yeah, she keeps it in the back room with old phone books in the drawer and extra plates and bowls on the shelves." Sam lived closest to Mom and Dad so she was most familiar with what they did and didn't have in the house and where it might be located.

"Oh, you mean the one they cut one leg shorter to sit on the baseboard?" Anne had been amazed when she saw that; but it evidently had been common to do this back in the mid to late eighteen hundreds. "Dad had to replace missing pieces, fix the tin doors and strip the paint off of the whole thing before getting it to look like what it originally did."

"Well, it's shaped kind of like that, a little shorter maybe," Kate informed them as she poured herself a glass of tea. "It has the drawer across the top like mothers and the doors in front, but it also has an opening on one end with a flap covering it where the cat enters and exits." Kate noticed her sisters had gotten everything out except the meat.

"Weird," Anne stated then continued. "Let's go look at it before we start dinner."

Kate barely got a glass of grape juice poured to take to Ell before her sisters headed for the door. "What's the big hurry? We've got all night don't we? I mean, we're not leaving until morning are we?" She had informed them by phone it was okay to leave.

"You know they'll want to leave early, which means we have to pack everything not necessary for the morning tonight and get it in the cars." Sam was talking as she walked ahead of her sisters, "I mean it's not like they expect everyone back to work right away."

"Yeah, but you know Dad will want to get as far as he can in daylight before stopping for the night," Anne offered. Heading home, she and Keith would branch off from the others halfway through the second day, Kate and Ell, would turn off an hour or so after that, while Sam and Todd would follow their parents' home before continuing on to theirs. They may all arrive at the beach at separate times at the beginning of the week, but leaving for home is a whole other animal.

"Correct as always," Kate stated, which got an angry look from her sister. "What," Kate replied questioningly, "Did I miss something while I was gone?"

"You know Larry, the guy covering for Keith until we return?" Anne was speaking very shakily and Kate put her empty hand on Anne's arm and told Sam to wait a minute. "His wife was in an accident this morning after church. Some jerk T-boned her car, she was six months pregnant with their first child; they had worked so hard to get pregnant. The baby is gone and his wife will be in the hospital for quite a while, the doctors don't think she will be able to have any more children."

"Oh Anne, I am so sorry ..." Kate's body began tingling all over.

Kate's grip on Anne's arm changed and she looked to see her sister with the calmest expression on her face. "What is it?"

Tears escaping the corners of Kate's eyes were leaving tracks down the side of her face. Removing her hand from Anne's arm she informed her sisters of a vision she had just experienced. "It was beautiful where she was, and the little girl was happy. She told me to tell them not to be sad, the doctors are wrong, they will have another child, a little boy and she will watch over and protect him all his life. She said her name was Ariel and she was glad she would be a big sister."

Anne's face was now pale, she had not told Kate the baby was a girl nor had she told her that the couple had only just decided to name her Ariel. This was a new branch in Kate's abilities that they had not known of before. Anne's look motivated Kate to answer the unspoken question.

"I didn't know I could either," Kate told them, "it may only be this once and that her spirit was still so strong."

"That was cool," Sam said, bringing everyone out of their dazed state. "You've got to tell the guys, and mom and dad will want to know."

"Let me digest it first, okay?" Kate wasn't sure she wanted everyone to know, she didn't want to tarnish the feeling it had left deep inside her; she was still tingling.

"Okay, but Anne will need to tell Larry and his wife when they get back," Sam stated.

"That's okay, but everyone else can wait for a while." Kate was adamant on this.

※

The girls finally arrived in the private parking lot and joined the men still checking the cabinet over themselves; they were amazed at its uniqueness. The front doors had punched tin to allow the pies to cool or in this case the litter box to breathe, plus gave you ample access to clean out the box. Being five foot wide and a foot and a half deep the cat had plenty of room to turn around in front of the litter box which faced the cat flap opening, not to mention, it allowed you to add a tray to catch loose litter off their feet. The extra container that held your fresh litter, fit perfectly behind the cat box on the opposite end for an easy refill.

It was a wonderful idea for a single cat home, but Kate wondered how it would work out with two. Unclipped males had a habit of marking any territory they feel might be invaded by another male or to let a female in heat know they are near. Kate had never intended on having more than one cat at a time, so she was kind of on shaky ground in this area. Would Blue mark his territory to protect Nellie from potential suitors? She hoped not and then maybe she would have Nellie fixed and that would take care of the problem, she would have to see how everything worked out first.

"This is so neat," Sam opened the doors and pulled out the drawer, checking everything out thoroughly. "You should have dad get measurements or at least look it over and maybe he can make some of these to sell."

"It would depend on if he could find the right size cabinets at the right price first." Todd wasn't sure you could find a lot of these cabinets in today's' market.

"No, I meant make his own from scratch," Sam informed Todd before continuing. "He can make them from barn siding, or probably any old wood building from the late eighteen to early nineteen hundreds."

"Do you really think he would want to be confined to making those things over and over?" Anne wasn't sure dad would like doing that.

"He could try one," Sam suggested, "that would let him know if he enjoyed it or not. I bet cat fanatics would pay a pretty penny for one of these. I'll see if I can find anything on the Internet that looks similar to this one when we get home."

"You better get Dad out here to look at it tonight," Anne informed them, "Or he'll have to drive to Kate's to look at it once we get home."

"Oh right," Sam replied, "I'll go see if they're back from their walk."

"I'm heading back to the kitchen," Kate said. "We've got to get started on dinner." All three girls headed back to the house. Sam continued through the house, went out the back door and took off down the beach in search of their parents while Anne and Kate began preparations. "I'm glad all we gave her to do was a simple spinach salad with raspberry vinaigrette, who knows how long she'll be out there."

"Too true, sister, too true," Anne replied as she washed her hands before she began cleaning the vegetables she would be sautéing with fresh rosemary, vegetable broth and olive oil.

Kate washed her hands before rinsing off the filet mignon, patting them dry and stacking them on a platter; at eight ounces each they had been their one big splurge. Locating a brush and the olive oil she headed to the door; turning toward Anne with the steaks piled so high on the platter in her hand that they threatened to topple over she asked, "Has that red velvet cake been cut into wedges for dessert?"

"Did it earlier, plus we went ahead and scooped the balls of butter pecan ice cream to add to it, they're covered in a bowl in the freezer," Anne told her without looking up from her vegetables, "*And* the honey pecan pieces to sprinkle on top are over there in a bowl on the microwave." She pointed with the end of her knife.

"You two did a lot while I was gone, thanks Anne. I'll be back up as soon as I get these on." Kate slipped out the side door and down the steps to the grill.

CHAPTER 36

▼

Sam came in the door off the deck, "I finally found them, lucky for me they were on their way back to the house. Dad said he would look it over but would make no promises." Sam washed her hands and filled a large bowl with vinegar water and thoroughly washed the baby spinach leaves as she asked half-heartedly, "I don't suppose either of you chopped the granny smith apples for me?" At the looks from her sisters she continued, "I thought not, well a girl can hope you know." Lifting the leaves out of the bowl she put them in a colander and dipped the colander several times in water before transferring them to paper towel to drain. "Do you think you will be able to talk to the dead again?"

Kate was chopping the leeks and fresh mushrooms for the Marsala mushroom sauce she would be fixing to pour over the steaks; she did not want to talk about anything serious right now. "We'll talk later; I still haven't had time to think it over, maybe while you massage my feet?"

"Thanks for reminding me I'm a loser," Sam whined as she washed the second apple.

"If you can't handle the consequences don't make the challenge," Kate quipped before continuing, "I just picked up on your aura."

"There you go, it was an unfair advantage," Sam complained, "I shouldn't have to pay; you were only one step ahead of me."

"Fine," Kate relented, "We'll let mother make the call."

"You might as well concede right now Sam, you know what mother thinks." Anne had tried to keep out of the squabble but knew mother's feelings on this subject; *a bet is a bet.*

All three sisters went silent at that. Kate headed downstairs to check the grill and returned with the progress. "The steaks will be done shortly let's get the rest of this finished so we can eat, I'm starved!"

☙

Blue and Nellie had been sleeping most of the day. She feared going home knowing nothing would be the same; she felt it deep inside and she snuggled up closer to the only thing that made her feel safe, Blue. He was her rock now; he was all she had left of this place. She shivered and it woke Blue from his sleep; he nuzzled her face and encouraged her to follow him downstairs.

Blue's female provider was in the kitchen cooking and he pestered her enough to give him some peanut butter. Nellie didn't like it, so she received a small bowl of cream, something Blue doesn't get because his body reacts unfavorably; so it is good to avoid it altogether. Besides, he preferred peanut butter anyway.

After the snack, they headed back up to the gallery and watched the activity down at Nellie's home. It was just as she feared, the police were crawling everywhere. Blue rubbed her face with his to let her know he cared. They stayed watching until darkness came and all was quiet on the beach. Blue noticed when they passed the bedroom to go back to the third floor that someone had brought Nellie's bed and carrier up. He took Nellie there and she fell into a deep sleep in her own bed, her muscles relaxed at the smell of familiarity; they began to unwind from the tenseness they had been in all day. She probably would sleep the rest of the night; Blue jumped up on the big bed and crawled under his fleece blanket, he too needed a good nights sleep.

☙

Everything was on the table except the salad. Sam waited until everyone was sitting down before tossing the vinaigrette dressing into the salad; doing it too soon would cause it to wilt. Placing the last salad in front of her; Sam asked Father to bless their food and ask for safe travels on their journey home tomorrow.

Keith and Ell ate their filet without the Marsala Mushroom sauce, while the rest of them smothered their steaks with it. The meal was excellent, the full bodied cabernet flowed freely and the girls promised a delicious dessert so no one overstuffed themselves before it was brought to the table.

This year with adults only at the beach, it had turned out to be quite enjoyable for all of them; with an added bonus of a mystery or two. Next year they would be back to argumentative teenagers, demanding grandchildren and endless sandcastles. But life happens and with it brings many changes, so how can you be bored?

CHAPTER 37

▼

They had been on the road for a little over two hours. It was a beautiful day and the cats had been climbing all over the litter hut when Blue found a loose board, leave it to him to find anything unusual. He had pulled at the board long enough that it moved, just enough for a human to see it was different. Blue was sure it had something hidden behind it; he could smell an odor other than the wood. He wiggled it to allow the crack to widen and ever so slightly a corner of paper showed. Blue was disappointed, it was only money, he knew because he had seen it in his human companion's purse before. He had been hoping for something else, something new or unusual to play with. Bored with his find he gave up and began slapping at Nellie's tail trying to get her to play.

Nellie had climbed on the wooden box to gain a better advantage when she stopped in mid-stride and cried a pitiful sound. She climbed to the front of the vehicle and jumped up into Kate's lap. Kate lifted Nellie up to look her in the face when she herself went white. Ell became alarmed and pulled the van to the side of the road thinking Nellie had hurt her in some way. By the time the van had stopped and he had turned off the engine, the color had returned to Kate's face and Nellie was jumping into the back to join Blue.

"Kate, what's the matter?" Ell wasn't sure what had occurred.

"I'm okay; just give me a minute will you?" Kate was trying to make sense of all the images that had hit her and was gone in an instant. It was unlike the experience she had had yesterday with Ariel; of which she still had not yet told Ell. Vera had come to see Nellie, but she didn't have the same presence Ariel had. Vera was being pulled into a dark place, a painful place with no love or light. Kate had felt the heaviness and prayed she would never experience it again.

"Don't leave me hanging," Ell insisted, bringing Kate's attention back. "We need to get back on the road, and you'll have to call your parents and let them know why we are no longer behind them."

"I'll explain everything while you drive." Kate was desperately searching for the right words to tell Ell when she blurted out, "but first I'll call mother." She dialed the number and waited for an answer as Ell started the vehicle and pulled back out into the flow of traffic. "Mother, we had a small problem with the cats; we'll catch up in a few minutes ... no, don't worry about us we're back on the road now; you were stopping at the same place in Tennessee weren't you? Okay, we'll see you then if we don't catch up before that." Kate hung up the phone and turned toward her husband, maybe he only needed the short version until they stopped for the night.

༺

Monday morning Sheriff Poole left the courtroom and headed toward his two deputies standing in the hallway with the prisoners, waiting on the elevator. There had been four people picked up over the weekend that had hearings this morning, two of them had been a drug bust, one was assault and battery on an undercover cop in drag, and the other was Vera Johnson.

As the Sheriff reached the group in front of the elevator it opened, and a man came barreling out yelling obscenities. He slammed into the Sheriff catching him off guard and causing him to catapult into the prisoners. Bodies scattered across the floor like bowling pins. The Sheriff recovered quickly, grabbing the man's arm and flipping him face down on the floor. He slapped the cuffs on the offender and turned to survey the damage. His deputies had gotten three of the prisoners to set up and lean against the wall to catch their breath. One prisoner was missing.

By this time the deputy viewing the camera monitors had came out into the hall. Sheriff Poole released the new offender over to the deputy and began his search for the missing prisoner. He headed first to the staircase, expecting an escape and anticipating a chase out the front door. But there was no need.

This person had been hit so hard they had tumbled backwards down the open staircase. Unable to stop their spiral decent due to the cuffs that shackled them, they rolled the full length of the marble steps, landing at the bottom in a heap. It was Vera Johnson, and her neck had been broken in the fall, the now permanent look on her face was one of shock.

Sheriff Poole's only thought: *now they would never find out about the deaths of all her husbands.*